SACRIFICE

HANNA WINTER
SACRIFICE

MANILLA

First published in Germany in 2012 by Ullstein Verlag GmbH, Berlin

First published in Great Britain in 2016 by Manilla Publishing
80–81 Wimpole St, London W1G 9RE
www.manillabooks.com

1 3 5 7 9 10 8 6 4 2

A CIP catalogue record for this book is available from the British
Library.

Ebook ISBN: 978–1–7865–8003–0
Paperback ISBN: 978–1–7865–8008–5
Trade paperback ISBN: 978–1–7865–8019–1

Typeset by IDSUK (Data Connection) Ltd

Manilla is an imprint of Bonnier Zaffre,
a Bonnier Publishing company
www.bonnierzaffre.co.uk
www.bonnierpublishing.co.uk

For James

'Memories make life more pleasant;
forgetting makes life more bearable.'
HONORÉ DE BALZAC

1

The rain ran down her face, her quick, springy footsteps bounced on the wet tarmac and her sweaty T-shirt clung to her back like a second skin. Dusk had already fallen when Lena Peters got back from her run and reached her front door in Boxhagener Street. Out of breath, she dropped to her knees for a brief rest. With her thoughts already on her meeting the next morning, Lena pulled her front door key out of the pocket of her tracksuit bottoms, then jogged through the inner court-yard lit only by the windows of the surrounding flats. Just a few metres from her ground-floor flat, she suddenly stopped in her tracks. A man in an anorak was standing by her bedroom window.

What the hell . . . ? Lena's pulse began to race. Gingerly she stepped closer and watched as the man peered into the lit-up room. He stepped over the terracotta planter into the small, bare plot behind the flat, which according to the estate agents was supposed to constitute a garden, despite its lack of plants. The man went over to the patio. Lena briefly considered calling the police, but then decided to deal with the situation herself. Just as she had always done.

Carefully, she picked up the small trowel that was leaning against the wall near the sandpit, and crept up behind him. The man seemed not to notice her, even though she was now close. He was about to slip his hand into the gap in the slightly ajar patio door when Lena struck him with the flat side of the trowel, square in the face.

'Get out of here or I'm calling the police!'

The man staggered back, groaning with pain and clutching his face as he fell backwards to the ground.

'Jesus, are you out of your mind?!' he snapped angrily at Lena, holding his bleeding nose. 'I *am* the police!'

Lena realised that she knew him.

'Herr Drescher? Volker Drescher?'

Horrified, Lena dropped the trowel and stepped closer. Shielded by the hood of his anorak was a slender man, in his mid-forties, with a gaunt look and a pointed chin. When he got to his feet, he was barely a head taller than Lena.

'For goodness sake, how was I supposed to know you'd—'

Drescher leaned against the wall, groaning as he set his glasses straight. He stared at Lena. 'For a woman of your build, you pack quite a punch!'

His response was no surprise; Lena knew people didn't expect much strength from her.

'Can I ask what you're doing here in my garden?'

'I rang the bell, but there was no answer. And when I saw that the light was on—'

'I never turn the light off when I go out.'

Drescher looked at her, surprised, but said nothing.

'Your nose – is it broken?' asked Lena, genuinely concerned.

He touched the bridge of his nose. 'No.'

Lena held her hand out to him, but Drescher ignored it. She watched as he composed himself and brushed the dirt from his anorak.

'Come on, I'll get you a plaster,' she said quickly. She turned to open the front door.

Shit! Shit! Shit! Did I really need to floor my new boss?!

'And perhaps a whisky, if you'd like – to help with the pain,' she added, waiting for Drescher to follow her.

Lena had chosen her small apartment primarily for the affordable rent. It was in an old building, but the flat hadn't been renovated and needed a lick of paint. The kitchen was right by the front door. Then there was the small dining room, which connected to the sitting room. At the end of the long corridor were Lena's bedroom, the bathroom and a tiny study. Apart from a few pieces of furniture, there was nothing to indicate what sort of person lived here. No family photos, postcards or holiday souvenirs. Not a single clue about her past.

Lena slipped off her damp trainers in the hallway, piled high with mostly unpacked boxes. Still a little dazed, she greeted her tabby tomcat, Napoleon, who wriggled between her ankles impatiently, meowing. Lena picked him up and gave him a little stroke.

'A nice place you've got here,' said Drescher. He pulled his hood back to reveal his light brown hair.

'Everything's a bit makeshift. I still haven't quite got round to unpacking.'

She put the cat down and led Drescher into the bathroom. In truth she couldn't imagine spending the next few weeks or months between these four walls. Although she had moved often, more or less of her own volition, she still found it hard to get used to new surroundings. But in the next few weeks she would probably only be coming home to sleep; the investigation into the ongoing series of murders – to which Drescher would be welcoming her tomorrow as the new criminal profiler, and which would keep them on their toes around the clock – was already keeping her pretty busy. Lena had been swotting up on the case; for days she'd barely had anything else on her mind.

'Where on earth were you, anyway?' Drescher asked, as Lena reached for a bottle of iodine, cotton wool and a plaster from the mirrored cabinet above the sink.

'I went for a run.'

'Damn it, Peters – I've been trying to call you. Didn't you have your mobile on you?'

Drescher was now standing right behind her. Lena, who was long accustomed to the curt tone taken by the police, turned around.

'No,' she said and dabbed his bloody nose with cotton wool doused in iodine, trying not to show that she was feeling nauseous and short of breath.

It always happened. Even just a few drops of blood evoked the memory of that day. Of the burning wreck of the car where she and her twin sister Tamara had been crushed in the back seat.

Blood.

Blood everywhere.

And smoke.

And shards of glass from the shattered windows.

Her mother lying unconscious on the passenger seat beside her father. And all the time the firefighters were trying to free Lena and Tamara from the wreckage, Lena clung to her mother's bloodied hand. She refused to let it go. Not even as the flames burst up around her mother. No sooner had the firemen dragged Lena from the debris, than the car exploded.

Help had come too late for her parents. The accident was around twenty years ago and yet, even after all this time, Lena still saw the blood on her hands.

'Why not?' asked Drescher, staring at her over his small glasses.

The question brought her abruptly back into the here and now. 'We agreed that I would come to HQ tomorrow morning and—'

'Tomorrow, tomorrow! Tell that to our killer!' He flinched suddenly. 'That stuff burns!'

Lena stopped dabbing and looked him straight in the eye. 'Another victim?'

Drescher's sigh spoke for itself.

'Tonight?' she asked.

'What, do you think this maniac only kills during office hours?' Drescher shoved his glasses up onto his hair, took the cool flannel that Lena handed to him and pressed it against his red, swollen nose.

'No, of course not . . .' she said calmly.

She couldn't afford to slip up again, if she wanted to preserve her last scrap of authority in Drescher's eyes. She suspected that Volker Drescher was the sort of policeman who had had to be persuaded to bring a profiler in on a case – because doing so proved that the investigation had reached a dead end. In most cases, Lena was only hired if the lead investigator had utterly failed to get anywhere, when the team's nerves were frayed and bringing in someone new was an act of desperation. She was quite used to being received with a mixture of suspicion and curiosity. This time, too, she knew she would be facing her new colleagues' glares boring into her neck as they tracked her every move, a critical eye on how she went about her work. But she'd developed a thick skin and enough confidence in her ability to shrug it off. At least that's what she told herself.

'Give me five minutes. I'll have a quick shower and be right back.' She handed Volker Drescher the plaster.

Drescher held up three fingers. 'Three minutes,' she heard from under the flannel. 'And if your offer still stands, I'd be glad of that whisky now.'

Lena stood smiling in the doorway. 'Help yourself. The bottle's on the kitchen table. There should be a glass somewhere.'

With that, she closed the bathroom door as Drescher headed towards the kitchen.

Moments later, Drescher placed two generously filled whisky glasses on the coffee table in the living room and sat down on the brightly coloured sofa, noticing as he did that it still had the crinkly protective covering on it. Drescher looked at his watch as the patter of the shower came from the bathroom. Eventually he picked up his glass and got up to look around. Bare walls, naked light bulbs, more removal company boxes. He peered into the open rooms as he walked past. A futon bed, an oversized desk with a laptop on it. The bookshelf was lined with hefty tomes about sex crimes and analysis of historical cases and court proceedings. He allowed himself a patronising grin when he spotted his latest book. *Let's see if she's got what it takes . . .*

Lena kept her eyes closed as she felt the warm water relax her neck. *Yet another victim. The intervals between the killer's attacks are getting shorter and shorter,* she thought as she turned off the water.

First there was a new victim every few weeks, then weekly, and now it's been barely three days since he last struck. With today's victim, that makes twelve women cruelly mutilated. She stepped out of the shower and dried herself quickly. *What is he trying to tell us?* She slipped on some clean knickers and a T-shirt, then pulled on her jeans. *Is he just flexing his muscles? Or is he getting carried away?*

Lena looked at the confused-looking woman in the mirror and quickly combed back her wet hair. She picked up her mobile, which she had left on the edge of the sink, and was just about to head back to the living room when she glanced at the screen. Confused, Lena stared at her phone for a moment before walking to the living room with the phone in her hand.

'You said you'd tried to ring me?' she said. 'That's weird, because there are no missed calls.'

'It was just a test,' said Drescher, his expression unchanged. 'I wanted to see how you'd react.'

A test? Lena wondered what was coming next.

Drescher cleared his throat. 'We're dealing with a brutal case, the likes of which we've never seen. And exceptional cases require exceptional measures, and exceptional qualifications, if you see what I mean . . .'

'What's your point?' Lena asked sceptically, as she sank into the leather chair opposite him.

'There are certain people who think this series of murders might be too much for you to handle.'

Lena felt her temples throb. 'But apparently you disagree, otherwise you wouldn't have brought me in.'

She noticed his glance down at her bare feet, then her flat chest and skinny shoulders. He then looked down at the glass of whisky and touched the plaster on his nose.

'You have an impressive academic background, Peters. And I don't just mean your outstanding marks in psychology and criminology, but above all your excellent research into criminal profiling.'

'Thanks.' A smile came to Lena's lips, and then quickly vanished. 'But you'd still rather your profiler was six foot – and built like a boxer,' she added, looking at his battered nose.

'Your words, not mine.' Drescher cleared his throat and pushed his glasses up with his middle finger.

Lena picked up her whisky from the coffee table and held herself back from emptying it in one swig. 'You yourself stated in an academic journal that good people are rare, and that it's as difficult to tell the competence of a team member from looking at them as it is to detect the motivation of a criminal.' The throbbing in her temples grew stronger as she felt a surge of rage come over her and she felt angry with herself for letting him get to her. To calm herself down more than anything, she stroked the soft fur of her cat, who had just jumped up beside her and was making himself comfortable.

Drescher cracked his knuckles and looked up from his glass. 'This is Berlin, after all – not Fischbach or whatever suburb it is you're from.'

How incredibly astute. 'If I may remind you, the red-light district murders, the dead children at the port and the poisoner were not in Fischbach either.'

'But this is completely different terrain,' he replied with a vehement shake of the head.

Lena held his piercing stare and wondered how she was supposed to convince him that she was right for the case. But did she even have to? After all, he was the one who had asked her to join the team, not the other way around. Lena washed away her irritation that he seemed to doubt her before she had even started work with a decent swig of whisky. Unexpectedly, she found herself smiling.

He wants to put me to the test? Fine, let him.

Lena gave the glass a shake and waited until she had his full attention. Then she closed her eyes and said, 'You're wearing a light blue cotton Ralph Lauren shirt with cuffed sleeves. It has six buttons, not including the one missing in the middle. In your right breast pocket is a charcoal grey Lamy pen, engraved with your name. It is slightly chewed at the end, perhaps because you're under pressure. You're not married. At least you haven't worn a wedding ring recently – there isn't the slight indentation you get over the years. Your Hugo Boss glasses have a small scratch at the front of the left arm, perhaps because you dropped them. You use Vetiver by Guerlain. Although this morning you only sprayed it behind one ear, most likely because you were in a hurry.' Lena kept her eyes closed. 'You value punctuality and you're clearly always punctual yourself, because,' she said, tapping her wrist, 'your watch is two minutes fast. You wear classic leather shoes, with heels a good four centimetres, which suggests that—'

'OK, Peters – that's enough,' Drescher interrupted. 'OK, you've won.'

When she opened her eyes again, she saw his astonished expression.

'I just wanted you to be warned, that's all,' said Drescher.

She stifled a grin and, for a moment, an oppressive silence hung like a deep abyss between them.

'I thought you lived alone?' Drescher asked abruptly, his eyes turned to a game of chess, which was set out on a plain white chest of drawers. 'Who's your opponent?'

Lena forced a smile. She didn't like to talk about herself. Besides, she didn't have the slightest desire to be interrogated by Drescher about her private life. She brushed his question aside with a shrug.

The abyss grew deeper.

She saw that Drescher was holding back a comment. He pulled a photograph out from the breast pocket of his shirt and placed it on the coffee table. Lena looked at the print and saw a young woman with a warm smile. She was wearing a short dress and high-heeled, strappy sandals. The picture was obviously taken at a party, and it looked like she was having a good time.

'The victim?' Lena asked.

Drescher took a deep breath. 'Her name is Yvonne Novak; twenty years old.' He bit his lower lip and shook his head. 'Barely more than a child.'

'Where was she found?'

'She hasn't been found,' he said, frowning. 'She's doing maths at Humboldt University and she disappeared without a trace after her lecture yesterday.'

Lena gulped, but for the time being she wanted to remain optimistic. 'That doesn't necessarily mean . . . She might have just left town. She could be anywhere.'

Drescher shook his head again and had a sip of his whisky. 'My instinct tells me it's related. Besides, yesterday she was supposed to pick up her brand-new car, a present from her parents

for doing well in her studies. A red Beetle with all the frills . . .
She chose it herself and according to her roommate she's been
looking forward to it for weeks. It's not the sort of thing you just
forget about, is it?'

'No, maybe not . . .'

'Ms Novak lives in a shared flat in Kreuzberg. Eyewitnesses
have on several occasions seen the same windowless black van
parked near the entrance door. A similar one was seen in the
area before the other victims disappeared.'

Lena put her glass down, annoyed. 'Why didn't you say so?'

'Good God, there isn't a single day when this accursed case
isn't dominating the headlines. We've already spent far too long
treading water in this investigation and we cannot allow there
to be any more victims. The press and the police chief are really
piling on the pressure.'

Lena pressed her lips together. 'Nevertheless, we still don't
necessarily need to assume the worst for Yvonne Novak.'

'No,' said Drescher. 'We don't.'

But Lena had the feeling there was something else was he
wasn't saying. That there was a crucial piece of information that
Drescher was holding back.

2

Just a few hours after she had fallen into bed, her mobile phone's ringtone tore Lena from a restless sleep. Her eyes half-shut, she fumbled about on the bedside table for the handset.

'Hi, Peters speaking . . .' Slowly she sat up and rubbed her sleepy eyes.

It was Volker Drescher. 'Damn it, where are you? There has been another victim. And it's almost certainly one of his.'

Lena suddenly woke up with a jolt. Pain hammered against her temples, which intensified after a quick glance at the alarm clock on the bedside table. It was eight o'clock – the meeting had already started! Lena shooed away Napoleon, who was lying curled up on the duvet, and jumped out of bed.

'I'm on my way!' she shouted into the phone. She had barely hung up when she clutched her head. *Shit, shit!* She never overslept – how could this have even happened? Cursing, she pulled off the baggy T-shirt she slept in, grabbed her bra and hopped with one leg in her jeans over to the wardrobe, while frantically trying to reconstruct the night before. The last thing she remembered was sitting up late with Drescher, discussing the case. And then? Lena paused. After Drescher had gone, she'd poured herself yet another whisky and eventually slumped into bed, exhausted. Lena massaged her temples. Her head felt as if a whole flock of birds was trapped inside her head. What was the matter with her? The only time that she had ever been so drunk that she couldn't remember anything was when she was a teenager, on the night of her prom. That was an eternity ago, and it was not at all like her to lose control. With a strange feeling in her stomach, she put on a dark blouse and buttoned it up to the top. She dashed into the bathroom, splashed some water on her face and tied back her shoulder-length, light brown hair. Her make-up was limited this morning to a smear of red lipstick, which she found made her look older and a bit more severe. Unlike her twin sister Tamara, Lena was more the sporty tomboy type, but today she opted for some heels, which made her a good five centimetres taller. A little spray of perfume, then she rushed into the kitchen and put some cat food out for Napoleon. In the hallway, she grabbed her bag and her trench coat from the wardrobe and ran out of the door. Lena put on her helmet, jumped onto her midnight blue Vespa and stepped on the accelciator. *Shit!* This would have to happen today of all days – her first day on the new job!

3

Barely twenty minutes later, Lena was rushing down the corridor to the meeting room, her heels clicking on the floor as she ran. The smell of freshly brewed coffee filled her nose, but there was no time for the dose of caffeine that Lena always started the day with. Her hand on the door handle, she paused a moment and took a deep breath before she opened the door. *Back straight, chest out.*

'From now on, no more details are to be passed to the press – and when I say nothing, I mean nothing! I hope I have made myself clear,' she heard Volker Drescher say, just before he spotted her. 'Ah, Frau Peters – how nice of you to join us,' he said. Drescher was facing his audience, leaning halfway across the table, and he cast an undisguisedly reproachful look at his watch.

'Good morning. I—' said Lena.

'Sit down.' He glared at her over the rim of his glasses, pointing to the nearest free chair.

Lena nodded as she looked around at the curious faces, and she immediately sensed the tension that was tangible in the room. Although the large windows were tilted open, there seemed to be a complete lack of oxygen in the air. Lena squeezed along the tight row of chairs before she sat down, her face flushed, repeatedly telling herself not to stare at the plaster on Drescher's nose or his bloodshot eyes. She paid as little attention to her new colleagues' glances as she did to the whispers. She rummaged about in her bag for her black leather-bound notebook and a pen, then tried to summon up a thoughtful expression as she followed Drescher's gaze as he turned to look at the wall covered in photos of all the women who, in the last two months, had been found mutilated. All twelve victims were found in fields, in wooded areas or on tucked-away stretches of the river bank, but not a single crime scene offered any usable evidence. The women in the photos were aged between seventeen and thirty-five, and each of them was naked and lying face down. Their hands were tied behind their backs. Each of them had had something severed from their body. One was missing her arms, another the genitals, another the entire bottom half of her body and one had even been decapitated. In addition to pronounced bruising, all the victims had numerous cuts as well as the typical bruising on the wrists and ankles that Lena had often seen on victims who had been abused when handcuffed. Besides these details, there was no dominant type among the women, no clear victim profile, as Lena had seen in the case of other serial killers, who, for example, targeted only blondes, redheads or brunettes, or particularly corpulent or frail women. *These women were as diverse as the social environments they came from*, Lena thought as she let her eyes roam over the photos. Lena gulped when she came to the last picture in the series. The maths student. The twelfth victim. Drescher was spot on the day before when he predicted it.

'The latest victim is twenty-year-old Yvonne Novak,' Drescher confirmed when he registered Lena's horrified look.

The young woman was also naked. The smile Lena remembered from the other photo had been replaced by an agonised, frozen look. When Lena saw that the woman's feet had been cut off, a shudder ran through her.

'A forklift driver found her body at the scrapyard in Wedding early this morning,' Drescher summarised again for Lena. 'According to the coroner, Yvonne Novak had already been dead for a good twelve hours by that point, from which we can assume that her murderer abducted her on Thursday, after her last lecture at the university.'

Immersed in thought, Lena nodded. 'Anything else?' she asked, surprised at the volume of her own voice. All eyes were now focussed on her.

Drescher nodded. 'Checks on Novak's laptop show that she'd been browsing forums on the occult, where they chat about black magic and all sorts of hocus-pocus,' he reported while everyone listened, transfixed. 'According to the chatroom logs, she had arranged to meet a certain "Dark Armon" early Thursday evening, about the time of her disappearance, in a bar in Görlitzer Strasse.'

Again the murmur of whispers got louder.

'Do we already know who's behind the screen name?' said Lena.

Drescher nodded. 'His real name is Ferdinand Roggendorf. Medical student, twenty-nine years old, no criminal record.'

'Please don't say he's related to that top lawyer from Charlottenburg?' groaned the redheaded guy sitting next to Lena, whose toned upper body showed through his tight polo shirt.

Drescher didn't flinch. 'Sorry to disappoint you, Vogt.' He cleared his throat sternly before he continued. 'Ferdinand Roggendorf is Richard Roggendorf's son.'

'Hmm, that's going to be fun . . .' sighed Vogt.

Hearing a slight groan from both sides, Lena turned to look at her colleagues. Most people in the conference room seemed to share Vogt's opinion: the displeasure about the person they would have to deal with was written clearly on their faces.

'According to witness statements, Novak never showed up in this bar in Görlitzer Strasse,' Drescher continued. 'Whether Ferdinand Roggendorf was there at the appointed time is yet to be established – questioning is still ongoing. So far, all we have been able to find out about him is that besides studying, he has a casual job as a ward assistant at Virchow Hospital –' Drescher pursed his lips – 'which is interesting, because according to the initial report from the coroner, there were confirmed traces of flunitrazepam in Yvonne Novak's blood.'

'Rohypnol – date rape drug,' Lena thought aloud. 'As a nurse, Roggendorf would have easy access to it.'

'Indeed,' said Drescher. 'At any rate, we'll have him under observation.'

Lena nodded pensively. *If this medical student was really on the chatroom to scout for potential victims, to meet them and knock them out with Rohypnol, we need to quickly establish if he was also in contact with the other women.*

'If his father gets wind of it, we're facing one lawsuit after another,' said Vogt. 'Anyway, I'm amazed this Ferdinand Roggendorf would have to moonlight as a nurse. I mean, with the fees his dad brings in, I'd have thought he wouldn't need to.'

'Perhaps Richard Roggendorf's a stingy bastard who wants his son to stand on his own two feet,' chipped in the lady with the head of brown curls sitting diagonally opposite Lena.

That must be Rebecca Brandt, thought Lena. Drescher had already told her about Brandt and described her as an indispensable member of the team. With her pink top, her plunging neckline and fake fingernails, she came across as more like your archetypal undercover investigator to Lena.

'Oh, before I forget: Roggendorf goes boxing every Thursday at seven p.m.,' added Drescher. 'The club's called The Steel Fist. Who wants to go and take a look?'

Vogt raised his hand and volunteered. 'I'll go. I know the club – you get some pretty nasty types hanging round there.'

'Very good,' said Drescher, as the door was pushed open from the outside and a plump woman entered.

'This has just arrived from Pathology.' She took two colour photographs out from an envelope and placed them on the table in front of Drescher.

'Thank you, Lucy.'

Before she had even left the room, Drescher pinned up the photos under the image of Yvonne Novak. These were close-ups of the lower legs, from which the student's feet had been severed.

'What do you notice?' Drescher asked the group.

It was obvious that it wasn't only Lena who would have preferred not to see such a sight early in the morning.

'Clean work,' remarked Rebecca Brandt. 'The same precision as with the other victims – the guy's no amateur.'

'If you ask me, we're dealing with a trophy collector,' mused Vogt, picking off a breadcrumb from his T-shirt. 'He's probably collecting the severed limbs in a fucking freezer somewhere – one I wouldn't want to stumble across—'

'I don't think so,' countered Lena. All eyes were now fixed on her again. 'Trophy collecting is a hobby. With a hobby, you have a kind of playfulness.' She turned her pen between her fingers. 'But whatever this psychopath's up to, he's not doing it for the sheer pleasure – no, he can't help it, he's obsessed.'

'The precision with which he cuts off the limbs – we could be looking at a surgeon,' Rebecca Brandt threw into the mix. 'One who, for example, has lost his licence and can't get back on his feet, but who knows what he's doing and is now making a killing running an illegal transplantation ring . . .'

'Then he would behave in a more professional manner,' Lena pointed out. 'He would dispose of the bodies properly. But these bodies were intended to be found, otherwise he would hardly have left them where they're so easy to find.'

'I'd agree with Frau Peters,' said Drescher.

The brunette leaned back and crossed her arms over her ample bosom. Lena saw a flash of irritation in her eyes.

Drescher's phone started ringing. After glancing at the number, Drescher took the call.

'Volker Drescher speaking. Yes?' He listened to the caller and Lena understood from the look on his face that this wasn't good news.

'I see . . . OK. That's fine, thank you.' Twelve pairs of eyes looked at him, transfixed, as Drescher hung up. 'A pedestrian has spotted a severed foot in the Spree quite near the junk-yard where Novak's body was found. The river police are in the process of cordoning off the whole stretch of riverbank and the police divers are still out looking for the second foot.' He squinted in Lena's direction. 'The foot is size thirty-nine, the same as Yvonne Novak. We'll see from the lab report whether it is indeed hers.' He turned back to the photo wall. At that instant, the plump Lucy burst into the room again.

'A young woman has just been found at Ernst-Reuter-Platz U-Bahn station,' she reported, in between short gasps for air, as she stared in horror at the fax she held in her hand. 'Her name is

Christine Wagenbach. Twenty-three. Kindergarten teacher,' she read aloud. 'From Schöneberg and she hasn't been to work for two days.' Lucy hesitated a second before she continued: 'Her right hand was cut off.'

No sooner had she uttered the words than a sudden commotion broke out.

Drescher banged his palm against the table. 'Fuck!'

4

Drescher took off his glasses, rubbed his eyes and put them on again. The conference room suddenly seemed even more stifling than before. Lena watched as Drescher's eyes quickly scanned everyone present and stopped at the brunette.

'Brandt, you head over to the morgue.'

Rebecca Brandt nodded. 'Sure.'

'No, no – she's still alive,' interrupted Lucy. For a moment there was dead silence in the conference room as everyone froze.

'My God!' Drescher exclaimed in shock. All of a sudden Lena saw how his face lit up.

'If this woman could identify the bastard—'

'They've taken her to the Franziskus Hospital, Budapest Strasse,' Lucy explained.

Drescher looked over at the plump lady. 'Is she conscious?'

'As far as I know.'

Volker Drescher was visibly nervous. 'Peters, you accompany Frau Brandt.'

Lena looked on in disbelief. 'With all due respect, the victim has just been found; questioning her so soon could adversely impact her recovery.'

Drescher looked into Lena's bright green eyes. 'You think it's too early to question her? Tell that to the next victim!'

Lena suppressed an indignant sigh. If Drescher had made a decision, it was apparently pointless to attempt to talk him round.

'All right, I'll speak to Christine Wagenbach, but I'll do it my way – and please, after everything she's been through, don't expect any miracles.'

Malicious rumour had it that Volker Drescher was a short-tempered bully with a bit of a Napoleon complex. He always insisted on getting his way and his often inappropriately irascible nature didn't fit with his slight physique. Lena was starting to realise what people meant.

'I'll expect your full report by tomorrow morning at the latest and the first draft of an offender profile within the next few days,' he said. And with that the discussion was over.

5

'I'm Rebecca Brandt. Call me Rebecca. Good to have you on the team,' the brunette introduced herself, holding her hand out to Lena as they walked quickly together along the corridor.

'Nice to meet you. Lena, Lena Peters.' Lena smiled and returned the firm handshake. Although still rankled by Drescher's orders, which seemed crazy to her, Lena tried to suppress her irritation.

'Let's take my car,' said Brandt as they stepped out of the headquarters. 'I'm parked right there.' She pointed her brightly painted fingernail at a metallic blue BMW 3 Series, which sparkled in the morning sun, and with her other hand she fished her car keys out of the pocket of her tight faded jeans.

'Nice car,' commented Lena as she got in on the passenger side. The smell of sweet perfume clung to the upholstery.

'So you're the new "psycho auntie",' said Brandt, clearly amused, as she started the BMW and drove out onto the street.

Lena raised her eyebrows. It was not unusual to find her job wasn't taken seriously. But Rebecca Brandt didn't seem to mean anything by it.

'If you like . . .' she replied, doing her seatbelt up.

'Drescher thinks highly of you.'

Lena looked at her and wondered if she was being serious.

'You're from Cologne?' Brandt asked.

'Yes, sort of,' Lena said hesitantly, appreciative that Brandt was talking to her so openly. 'I'm originally from Fischbach, a small town nearby. But I studied in Cologne.'

'I had a thing in Cologne with a property shark, he was a big fish in the industry – though with a bit of a small tail,' said Brandt and laughed. 'And, as it turned out, he was also still "happily" married.'

Lena also had to laugh.

'I'm living on my own at the moment, which is probably for the best with this job,' said Brandt as she turned off towards Charlottenburg. 'And you?'

'Me?' The question caught Lena off guard. 'Me too.' She gave a reserved smile and turned to look out of the window. If she were honest with herself, she could barely remember what it was like to be with a man. She just wasn't the type for making strong commitments. Since her break-up two years ago with Matthias, whom she knew from university, she was cautious of letting anyone get too close. She was afraid of leaving herself vulnerable. *You can't be left on your own if you're already alone.* That was her credo, even if she wouldn't exactly recommend it to anyone else.

'You said I'm the *new* psycho-auntie?' Lena changed the subject.

Brandt nodded and looked ahead at the road. 'Before you we had Dr Dobelli, but she chucked it in.'

This was news to Lena; Drescher hadn't told her anything about a predecessor. 'And why did Dr Dobelli leave?'

'I don't know,' replied the police officer with a shrug. 'She just went underground during the investigations and never resurfaced.'

Worried, Lena turned to Rebecca. 'And that wasn't followed up?'

'You'll have to ask Drescher yourself.' Rebecca braked sharply at a red light. 'But between you and me: Dobelli was a cranky old cow and most of us were glad to see the back of her.'

Lena could see on Rebecca's face that there was more behind this story, but decided not to ask.

'Can you ever get all this sick shit out of your head?' Rebecca changed the subject. 'Drescher told me you've spent more time in high-security psychiatric institutions, studying the psyche of serial offenders, than most police cadets spend at the academy.'

Lena smiled. 'Maybe, I don't know,' she said, staring through the windscreen. 'I guess the abysses of the human soul hold a kind of fascination for me.'

Rebecca shook her head sceptically. 'It's a tough one, this case, but for me, as an investigator, it's all about the evidence.'

Lena nodded, not saying anything. For the rest of the journey she was only half-listening. In her head, she was already thinking about the questions she would ask the victim. This was no ordinary textbook situation. Lena had her very own strategy.

6

As the glass doors of the entrance to the Franziskus Hospital slid open, Lena felt a nauseous sense of unease. She hated hospitals. And as she followed Rebecca Brandt in silence along the long corridor, which smelled of disinfectant, she wasn't sure what was making her stomach turn more: the thought of the interview she was about to conduct or the images of back then, memories that were stirred up as they passed signs to Intensive Care and the Emergency Burns Unit. Although Lena had tried to arm herself inwardly against such thoughts, the memories welled up in her like an uncontrollable need to throw up. She had just steadied herself when a door was thrown open and several nurses shoved past wheeling a blood-streaked young girl. Lena felt a choking sensation at the sight of her. And yet she couldn't take her eyes off the girl and she watched, lost in thought, as they hurried away along the corridor. Every fraction of a second, another fragment of memory flashed through her mind like lightning. She looked down at her hands and suddenly pictured the blood from the car accident. As had happened so often before, Lena had to force herself to resist the impulse to rush to the bathroom and scrub her hands clean.

In the lift she felt tense and, when Brandt introduced herself and Lena at the nurses' station, Lena prayed that her unease would not be obvious.

'Hello. My name's Brandt, Homicide.' Rebecca Brandt stood confidently in the entrance to the ward, pulled out her badge and pointed to Lena with a nod. 'This is my colleague, Lena Peters – a psychologist working with us on the case. We would be grateful if we could speak with Ms Wagenbach.'

'From the police . . .' echoed a plump, older ward sister, who was just about to go through the shift schedules with two other nurses. She came up to them with a suspicious expression. 'I don't think Frau Wagenbach is ready to be questioned.'

'I completely understand, Frau –' Brandt glanced briefly at the sister's name badge – 'Frau Plötz. But we are investigating a series of murders and—'

'The patient's condition is extremely unstable,' announced the tired-looking doctor who had just entered the nurses' station. 'Frau Wagenbach needs peace and quiet. If the patient's statement is so important, then I'm sure you'll be able to wait until tomorrow.'

'Ms Wagenbach is our only witness,' Lena joined in, turning to the doctor with a trusting smile. 'We are fully aware of our responsibility to the patient, but I'm afraid tomorrow could be too late for the next victim.'

The doctor and the ward sister exchanged glances. 'All right, come with me,' she sighed, and she led the sister, Lena and Brandt to Christine Wagenbach's room.

'That's her room over there,' the sister clarified and went on ahead. Lena and Brandt followed her along the corridor.

'The patient has only just come round from anaesthesia. We had to give her a shot of a pretty strong painkiller. I'd assume she's still a bit out of it.'

'Are they Wagenbach's parents?' Lena asked, looking over at an older couple who were sitting in the waiting area.

The man had his arms wrapped firmly around his wife, while she had her face buried in her hands, her sobbing ringing out across the hall.

'Yes,' the sister answered quietly. 'The mother hasn't been able to bring herself to go over to her daughter yet.'

When Lena and Brandt opened the door to the room, Christine Wagenbach was half propped up in bed. Lena paused a moment in the doorway. All the tubes and machines. Again she forced herself to suppress thoughts of back then and to focus on what lay ahead. Wagenbach was wearing a light blue hospital gown. Her eyes were only half-open, staring out of the window, and she didn't seem to notice Lena, Brandt or the nurse. Her face was ashen. Her dry lips were slightly open.

'Frau Wagenbach, there is someone here from the police . . .' the nurse announced timidly and motioned to Lena and Brandt to have a seat on the chairs next to the bed.

When the young woman didn't respond, the sister turned to Lena. 'Ten minutes,' she said, 'that should be enough.' She closed the door quietly on the way out.

They sat in silence a moment, before Lena cleared her throat. 'Frau Wagenbach, my name is Lena Peters. I'm a psychologist and I work for the homicide division . . . I can't imagine how awful everything you've gone through must have been,' she began cautiously, trying not to let her gaze fall or to think about the stump that lay beneath the blanket instead of her right hand.

'Would you be willing to answer a few questions for us?'

The woman did not move, just continued to stare out of the window.

Rebecca Brandt shifted her position on her chair. 'What did the guy look like?' she suddenly blurted out.

Lena's head snapped around to face her and she put a finger up to her lips. 'You don't have to break the door down!' she hissed at Brandt and asked her to wait outside.

The policewoman threw up her hands. 'As you wish,' she whispered and left the room.

Lena waited until she had closed the door before she turned to Christine Wagenbach with an apologetic look. 'I was told that you're a kindergarten teacher . . .' she began again. 'That must be a lot of fun . . .' she said with a smile. 'I love children.'

No reaction.

It's too soon! It's much too soon to start questioning her! It's just going from bad to worse this morning! thought Lena angrily. First she was late for the meeting, then she learned on the way that her predecessor had mysteriously disappeared during the investigation, and now this premature interview of an utterly traumatised victim!

Lena decided to start again. She leaned forwards slightly and rested her elbows on her knees. 'First of all, I want to express my sincere sympathy for what has happened to you,' she continued, trying to capture a warm, soothing tone. 'I can only imagine how you must feel.'

All of a sudden the young woman turned her head to face her, as if in slow motion. 'There's no way you can imagine!' Her voice trembled and broke off. 'You haven't got the slightest idea how it feels to be attacked by such a monster!'

Lena sat there and didn't flinch. Wagenbach wasn't to know about her past. About the humiliation and torment she had endured back then, which had turned her into the lone wolf she was now. Not even a trained observer would have noticed the vulnerability that lay behind Lena's serious façade, which only peeked through at fleeting moments of weakness.

Lena looked at the young woman for a moment and took a deep breath. 'Despite the terrible things that have been done to you, you had a guardian angel looking over you,' she continued. 'As I'm sure you know, there were other women who didn't – women who didn't manage to escape.' She paused, allowing her words to sink in and hoping to catch the young woman's eye again. 'The police are doing everything in their power to catch the man who did this to you. But we need your help, Frau Wagenbach, so that he cannot ever hurt you or any other woman ever again.'

Christine Wagenbach hesitated before she managed a barely perceptible nod.

'Thank you. Then I'll ask you a few questions.' Lena reached down to her handbag to pull out her black notebook. 'Have you been using any online chatrooms lately?'

'No, never.'

Lena nodded before she carried on with her questions. 'You were found in a tunnel in the U-Bahn,' she said, advancing calmly and objectively. 'Do you remember how you got there?'

A frightened shake of the head.

'Please take your time before you answer. You have all the time in the world.'

Unlike us.

'Or could you perhaps tell me where you were when you—'

'I was . . . I was on my way to work, on my bike, just like every morning,' the woman spoke up suddenly. Her voice was little more than a hoarse croak.

Lena saw her lower lip tremble. 'Take your time,' she reassured the patient in a hushed voice. 'You're safe now; nothing will happen to you here.'

Tears ran down Christine Wagenbach's cheeks and it was a while before she was able to proceed.

'On the way I stopped at the small bakery where I always get my breakfast . . . I parked my bike and went inside . . . but when I came out again, someone had thrown my bike into the bushes a few metres away. I . . . I looked around, but there was no one there . .' Her words were now increasingly clear.

'And then what happened?'

'I went over to pick up my bike . .' She stopped a moment, remembering what happened. Small beads of sweat gathered on her forehead. 'Then I suddenly felt a sharp pain in my neck . . . I wanted to turn around but by then it was too late – I collapsed . .'

He injects his victims with something to knock them out before he abducts them, Lena noted down, then looked up again. 'And when you regained consciousness?'

'Everything was so strange and blurred . . . There were all these bright lights, so I could hardly see . .' Wagenbach blinked as though the light was still stinging her eyes. 'I was strapped down . . . on a table.'

Lena closed her eyes. Just the thought of what had been done to the women sent a shiver down her spine.

'I was wearing a . . . a mask, I think it was an oxygen mask, connected to a kind of machine . .'

Lena made another note in her book, although secretly she would have preferred to spare herself and Wagenbach the gruesome details.

'I was scared. Jesus, I was scared! And then suddenly there was this man.'

Lena held her breath. 'What did he look like?'

'I don't know . . . He was wearing a kind of surgical gown . . . and a mask and—'

'So you couldn't see his face?'

Hesitantly, Wagenbach shook her head.

That would have been too good to be true.

'He . . . he had a syringe in his hand,' the young woman continued. 'Oh God, he . . . he came at me with it! And I . . . I couldn't do anything!'

Suddenly Lena saw Wagenbach begin to tremble, seized again by the same terror.

'And before I knew it, I was suddenly . . . kind of paralysed . . . I had no control over my body. And then there was noise and all this blood!' She tossed her head left and right, as though trying to shake off the agonising sound.

Lena felt an icy shudder. She had to really force herself to continue listening, while at the same time wondering if Christine Wagenbach was indeed capable of realising the full extent of what had been done to her. Whether she had in fact realised that at that moment her hand had been severed, that she would be maimed for the rest of her life.

'You're doing well, really well, Frau Wagenbach,' Lena spoke to her gently, rising from her chair to wipe the sweat from her brow with a tissue.

'And then this pain,' Wagenbach added, sobbing. 'This excruciating pain!'

Lena looked up from her notes, confused. For a moment she thought she had misheard. 'Just a second – after this injection you weren't unconscious but awake the whole time?'

Slowly, very slowly, the young woman lifted her eyes. 'Yes.' The tears were now streaming from her eyes. 'I was wearing a kind of . . . like a mask, I think it was an oxygen mask . . . And I . . . I could feel everything, but I couldn't move an inch.'

Lena stared, stunned, and needed a moment to process what she had just heard. Gradually it dawned on her: *the fucking sadist had injected her with alcuronium chloride!*

7

'And what happened after that?' Lena asked, her voice husky after a long pause.

'I . . . I don't know . . . I must have passed out . . .' Lena could see how hard she was thinking.

'I don't know how long it was until I came back round, but it seemed like for ever,' she said in a whisper, while her red-rimmed eyes filled again with tears. 'I was lying on the floor in a windowless room . . . I think it was a basement.'

'Frau Wagenbach, I can imagine that it must be extremely difficult for you, but please try to describe this basement room for me.'

The young woman looked at her, eyes wide with fear. She swallowed before she said, 'This awful pain . . . I could . . . could hardly take in anything else . . . except . . .'

'Except?' asked Lena.

'I could hear insects buzzing everywhere. Hundreds of flies were crawling on a red puddle on the floor . . . And on the walls were all these photos . . .'

'Photos?'

When Lena saw that the young woman was having trouble keeping her eyes open, she realised that she needed to press on. 'What kind of photos were they, Frau Wagenbach?'

Christine Wagenbach thought hard. 'I ... I'm not sure, but I think they were of women ... women I'd seen before somewhere . . .'

The women he had already mutilated! The thought shot through Lena's head. She made a note and looked up again. Wagenbach shook her head in disbelief, as if she had still not grasped that she herself had become part of this horror.

'And I think all the pictures had a . . . a red cross on them.'

He crosses them out as soon as he kills them, Lena noted down.

'And then there were some more photos.'

Lena's eyebrows shot up in surprise. 'What were they of?'

Wagenbach pressed her eyelids shut, then opened them again. 'More . . . women . . .' she continued, her voice weak now. 'But they didn't have a cross on them . . .'

Dumbfounded, Lena looked at her notes. *Oh dear God, he already has his sights set on his next victim!*

She forced herself to remain calm, not to let Wagenbach sense her horror. 'And what happened next?'

'I wanted to get up, but everything was spinning before my eyes, like . . . as if I were on drugs. And then . . . then I . . . I ripped the sleeve off my jumper so I could bandage up the wound.' She looked up. 'I mean the wound . . . on my right arm.'

Lena stared at her face. She still seemed not to have understood.

'And then . . .' she continued, 'then somehow with my last bit of strength, I dragged myself up with my shoulder against the wall . . . I fell against the door, which was open by a crack – the bastard obviously didn't expect me to come round so quickly . . .'

Whatever he gave her for the op, he must have got the dose wrong, Lena realised. *Which would suggest that he's perhaps not as much of a genius when it comes to anaesthetics as he'd like to believe – or perhaps he's started getting sloppy and making mistakes.*

'And then what happened?'

'I paused by the door to make sure the coast was clear. But then I heard his voice . . .'

Lena looked up and had the feeling she was on the home straight to the finish line. 'And what did he say?'

'I didn't hear any . . . any clear sentences, more a kind of . . . mumbling.'

'Frau Wagenbach, do you think you would recognise his voice?'

Please say yes. Please tell me you could identify him from his voice!

The woman nodded. Hesitantly, but she nodded.

Excellent.

'And was the other person also male?' She saw how the young woman's pupils jumped about restlessly under her drooping eyelids.

'No, there wasn't . . . I think he was alone . . . He was talking to himself . . . And then suddenly everything went silent,' she continued so quietly that Lena had trouble following her words.

'I heard him go up some stairs. I assumed he was gone . . . so I took a deep breath and dragged myself out of that chamber . . . My legs were so heavy . .' Her breath quickened. 'I ran and ran, through this endless, long corridor . . . It was all narrow and stuffy, I could hardly breathe. There were flies buzzing everywhere . . . and there were display cabinets a metre high, full of glass containers with murky liquid in them, with . .' Her face twisted into a look of disgust and her voice trailed off.

Lena shuddered as the penny dropped. *He preserved them? But why? Are we dealing with a pathological collector after all? No, that would be too straightforward. If it was simply about expanding his collection, he would hardly be so meticulous in his choice of victims.*

She wrote quickly to get everything down. 'Was there anyone else in the cellar besides you?'

'I don't know. But suddenly I heard him coming back. I heard his footsteps behind me. My God, he must have followed the trail of blood . . . He was getting closer and I was sure that it was only a matter of time before he caught me. And then suddenly I was out, in the yard.'

'What did the yard look like?' asked Lena.

'I don't know . . . I didn't see much – as soon as I realised he had followed me into the yard, I hid behind a skip and was just praying that he wouldn't find me. After a while, I lost sight of him . . . Then I started running, I just ran and ran . . .'

Lena felt like her heart had missed a beat. 'Did you see his face?'

The young woman nodded, in a daze. 'Yes . . . in the yard . . . and this time he wasn't wearing the mask . . .'

Lena felt like clapping her hands with glee. 'Can you describe him to me?'

'He . . . he . . .' She tried to force the words out, but her voice broke up.

'Frau Wagenbach, please try to think: what did he look like? Did he look familiar to you?'

'No.' She shook her head before continuing. 'I kept running . . . I just ran and ran . . .'

Lena sensed that she was on the verge of losing her. Christine Wagenbach apparently had some kind of mental block when it came to speaking about her tormentor.

Lena glanced at the clock and said, 'Frau Wagenbach, please try to recall what the man looked like. Every detail could be enormously important.'

Lena had barely said this before Wagenbach tried to straighten up in bed. *No – shit!* With lightning speed, Lena snapped her notebook closed and jumped up to help her. But it was too late. Her eyes wide with sheer terror, the young woman stared at her right arm, at the point where instead of her hand there lay only a bandaged stump.

'My hand! My hand!' she screamed. It was as if until this point she had still hoped to wake up from this nightmare. It was precisely as Lena had feared.

'Stay calm, Frau Wagenbach.' She was by now completely hysterical and would not stop screaming. Lena's pulse was racing. Her eyes flicked over to the ECG monitor which was beeping manically. Lena ran out into the corridor to call the duty nurse, who was already rushing towards her with the doctor and the two nurses. The nurse glared at Lena and pushed her aside as she stormed into the hospital room after the senior consultant.

'I didn't mean for this to happen!' protested Lena.

'A sedative, quickly!' she heard from the room before the door closed.

'What happened?' asked Rebecca Brandt, who had been waiting with Wagenbach's parents in the hallway and jumped up to join her. But before Lena could reply, Wagenbach's mother ran over.

'What have you done?' she shouted at Lena.

'Nothing, nothing at all!' Lena defended herself, holding her palms out defensively.

'Come on – it's probably best we go,' suggested Brandt, tugging Lena gently on the sleeve. But Lena had no time to react.

'If anything happens to my daughter because of this, I'll hold you personally responsible!' cried Wagenbach's mother, hitting out at her. 'You monster, leave us alone!'

Lena ducked and held her hands up in front of her face. As Rebecca Brandt and Christine Wagenbach's father tried to hold the mother back, the door to the patient's room opened.

'We've given your daughter a light sedative. She's calm for the time being,' said the doctor, at which point Wagenbach's mother stepped away from Lena and fell sobbing into the arms of her husband.

Thank goodness, thought Lena. Her cheeks glowing, she stood up and smoothed down her trench coat. She was thoroughly shaken, and when Christine Wagenbach's parents disappeared into the patient's room, she followed Brandt at a brisk pace to the lift, to head back to HQ.

But phew – it went well! Lena could hardly believe how far she had managed to get.

'If looks could kill, you'd be dead right now,' Brandt hissed as they stepped into the lift. As soon as the doors had finally closed behind them, Lena dropped her head back and let out a deep breath.

'So?' asked Brandt.

Lena looked at her, but she still needed a moment to compose herself. 'Drescher should be pleased,' were the words that came, reluctantly, to her lips.

Brandt nodded. 'I just had a little chat with the parents. The father said that, when they brought her in, she was jabbering away about some music.'

'Music? What sort of music?'

Brandt shrugged. 'Sounds like there was an opera playing in the cellar . . .'

Lena frowned. 'She didn't say anything to me about it . . . Did her father know which opera it was?'

'No, sadly.'

Lena watched the electronic display scroll through the numbers of the floors.

'But anyway, how did it go?' Brandt probed impatiently.

'The good news is: Wagenbach saw him.'

'That's fantastic! And could she describe him?'

'No, not yet. I guess we need to give her some time,' sighed Lena. 'I'll try again tomorrow.'

Brandt looked at her quizzically. 'And the bad news?'

'He's got photos of the victims on the wall, and alongside them are some other women – presumably his next targets.'

'Shit.'

Lena nodded in agreement. With a serious expression, she looked Brandt straight in the eyes. 'It would appear we're dealing with a sadist whose perversion and ruthlessness knows no bounds.'

'How do you mean?'

'He injects his victims with alcuronium chloride.'

Brandt shrugged. 'Never heard of it.'

The doors of the lift opened on the ground floor.

'It's a South American arrow poison that triggers a temporary paralysis of the entire muscular system. However this muscle relaxant has no effect on the patient's consciousness or sensation of pain – but as the tongue is paralysed, it is impossible for the victim to scream.'

For a second Rebecca Brandt remained rooted to the spot in the lift, and as Lena turned around to her, the colour seemed to drain from her face.

'Are you saying that during the amputation the women were fully conscious and able to feel everything?'

Lena nodded. 'I'm afraid so.'

'Fuck me. That's disturbing.' Brandt walked quickly after her. Lena waited until she had caught up with her before they continued to speak at a hushed level so that the patients in the corridor wouldn't overhear.

'It turns out he doesn't kill his victims straight after the amputation either, but leaves them alive for a while.'

Brandt grimaced. 'But why?'

'Well, if we knew that, we'd probably be making a lot more progress. I'm going to call a meeting for early tomorrow morning,' said Lena, looking at Brandt with a gloomy expression. 'We can only hope that won't be too late for one of the women in the photos.'

8

If there was anyone who understood him, then it was Gemmy. And Gemmy didn't ask any questions. Ever. With him he could be who he was deep inside: Artifex. The gifted artist. The master. The judge over life and death. But when he saw the boy like this – sprawled out on his front, stark naked, on the shabby mattress in the back room of his junk shop, with the PlayStation console in one hand and a bottle of beer in the other – he couldn't help but let out a sigh of regret. How nice it would be to take Gemmy with him one day, to let him take part in real life, which had so much more to offer than his tedious shoot-'em-up games. More than once he was inclined to let Gemmy share in his blood-drenched fantasies in practice, not just in theory. But Gemmy simply couldn't keep his hands off the accursed drugs, which made him unpredictable at times, and Artifex could not allow anything in the world to endanger his mission. Not until he had completed his masterpiece – his dream since he was a boy. After all, what are dreams for if not to make them come true? Leaning his shoulder against the doorframe, Artifex's gaze drifted slowly over Gemmy's shapely backside, over his slender, delicate back and up to the closely shaven hair on the back of his head. Gemmy was a good boy and brought him a lot of pleasure. It was just the needle scars on his forearms that increasingly worried him. Gemmy ran away from home at the age of fourteen and since then he'd earned a living as a rent boy on Jebens Strasse. Unlike the stereotype, Gemmy came from a good family, but for reasons that only he knew, he didn't want to go back there under any circumstances. It was well known that nothing was off limits with him. But that wasn't the only reason Artifex invited him so often to the back room of his shop. Often he didn't even want sex. Gemmy seemed to be the only person who didn't judge him for his dark fantasies. And since Gemmy didn't read the newspapers or watch the news, he could be pretty sure that the boy would never know that he'd actually been living out his murderous cravings.

Oh, Gemmy . . . Once again he had to bite his tongue and keep his excitement about his forthcoming spree all to himself.

9

Tomorrow afternoon, straight after the press conference scheduled for the release of a new US blockbuster at the Ritz Carlton, he would make his next strike. His chosen target was not a celebrity, however. It was a petite reporter who had awakened his interest the other day in a cafe on the Simon-Dach-Strasse. She had sat at the next table and spoken so loudly on the phone that it had been almost impossible not to listen to her conversation. Not just for him, in fact – everyone at the surrounding five or six tables. The reporter seemed to be pretty new at her job and was showing off on the phone that she was going to be interviewing some pumped-up action hero at the press conference. Afterwards, she would drive back to the office to bash out the best questions and answers to post online before her competitors could beat her to it. Artifex couldn't help but smile. Obviously proud of herself, she had trumpeted her good news in glorious detail to everyone in the cafe. But it wasn't actually what she said that caught his attention – no, it was her unconventionally curvaceous mouth that fascinated him, distracting him to the extent that he almost forgot for a moment that he was in the middle of a cafe. The sharply curved, slightly downward-pointing lips lent her a somewhat defiant look. Artifex had to really force himself not to stare at her; the lips were just perfect and would give his work that special touch he had so long been looking for. How was the airhead to know that she would never get to write her article?

Tilla would be very pleased with his latest accomplishment.

Artifex felt a trickle of sweat running down his back. In his mind he pictured the petite reporter laid out in front of him on the operating table, tied down by her arms and legs. Gradually she would come round and stare at him with terror-stricken eyes, begging him for her life as he prepared her next injection and got ready to make a start on the amputation. Artifex forced himself to push the image out of his head, as he still had a lot to prepare before tomorrow. He walked over to the sparsely furnished kitchenette, took down some vials of acetone, formaldehyde and hydrogen peroxide from the filthy kitchen cabinet, pulled the plastic bag containing the latex gloves and scalpels out from under the sink and shoved everything into his rucksack.

'I'm going out. I'll spend the evening with Tilla – I think she's quite lonely out there.'

'Mmhm . . .' murmured Gemmy, still focussed on his computer game and on emptying a whole magazine of bullets in some gangster's chest.

With a slight smile, Artifex again let his eyes glide over Gemmy's body. 'Will I see you tomorrow?'

'Dunno . . . maybe . . .'

'About the same time as usual? I'd like that.'

Suddenly Gemmy yanked his head around and glared at him with angry, bloodshot eyes. 'Can't you see I'm busy? And you're my not my fucking dad, all right?' Without waiting for a response, he turned back to face the screen, to carry on pumping lead into the guy.

Artifex swallowed. 'Fine, whatever you say . . .'

Gemmy hated nothing more than feeling hemmed in, he knew that. And it hurt him inside. Just the thought that one day Gemmy might not come back stabbed him in the heart – like a stray cat, which visits occasionally and you feed it and grow fond of it, but then it spurns you all of a sudden. He had for some time even toyed with the thought of putting Gemmy up along with Tilla in the basement workshop. But he was sure Tilla wouldn't be happy about it. She had always been very wilful, even if she was a good soul deep down. He went into the bathroom and turned on the light – a bare bulb hanging from the low ceiling. He picked up the comb from the dirty sink edge and dragged his blond wavy hair into a meticulous side parting, gazing into the cracked mirror with his radiant blue eyes and smiling to himself. With his distinctive facial features and his broad shoulders, he certainly couldn't complain about his appearance. And on top of that, the new jacket he'd just got in the sales looked pretty good on him. Tilla always said he had a movie star face, but he thought that was a bit of an exaggeration. Especially as a movie star would hardly be likely to run a junk shop. The second-hand tat they sold had never particularly been his thing, but his older sister Tilla loved the shop, so to this day he didn't have the heart to sell up. And since the lease for his two-roomed apartment in Wedding had been terminated, he lived in the back room behind the shop. Besides all the trash they sold, they also stocked a few Berlin souvenirs, which brought the odd errant tourist their way and topped up their income so it was just enough to make ends meet. And every now and then he sold one of his own macabre artworks, which he worked on night after night in his basement workshop he rented 'for special purposes' in north-east Spandau.

Thanks to a Russian gallery owner who exported his works worldwide, his sales had developed into an increasingly lucrative business. Feeling wistful, he placed the comb on the edge of the sink and went back to Gemmy in the back room.

'Just pull the door behind you if you go,' Artifex shouted as he left the shop to go and seek out an old acquaintance, a beefy security guard who was in charge of security at press conferences and who owed him a favour.

10

When Lena and Rebecca Brandt got back to the office at noon, Volker Drescher was out. Lena spent the rest of the day behind her desk, evaluating Wagenbach's statement. Lena's office was rather spartan. A desk. An office chair. A filing cabinet. An empty bookshelf. That was it. As with her apartment, there was absolutely nothing here that said anything about its occupant. Originally Drescher had set aside another large room for Lena, with big windows and a view over the park. But it was right next to the coffee area, and the constant comings and goings of colleagues and the irritating clatter of dishes would have been detrimental to Lena's ability to concentrate. She preferred to have peace and quiet when working and had therefore opted for a more secluded office, which was significantly smaller.

She was tired and still a little shaken from the morning's interview at the hospital. That evening she needed a hot bath and a glass of wine to go over it all again. But there was still plenty of time until then. Lena spent the next few hours reviewing all aspects of Christine Wagenbach's statement. Afterwards she drafted her first attempts at a profile of the offender and prepared for the team meeting the next day, where she would present her thoughts about how to proceed in the case, before they went to pay Christine Wagenbach another visit in hospital.

It was shortly after 9 p.m. when Lena left her office. She took the lift down to the archives to look up the case file of her predecessor Dr Dobelli. It was pleasantly cool in the basement, although the air was as stale and dusty as the investigation files, which were full of the blackest depths of the human soul and lined up on endlessly long shelves. An ancient neon light flickered and hummed softly to itself. Lena needed a while to get her bearings. The clicking of her heels echoed along the aisle until she stopped to face the shelf she needed.

'Danner, Decker, Dirksen, Dobelli – ah, here we are,' she muttered, pulling out the file. As she opened the brown cover, however, she found that the contents were missing. Lena frowned. *Someone's removed the file* . . . Lena was just about to put the empty folder back when she heard a soft laugh. She also noticed the smell of cigarette smoke.

'Hello? Is anyone there?' Her heart pounding, Lena walked to end of the aisle.

'Charlie, you're still here?' The archivist, who she had met that morning in the hallway, was sitting in his little cubbyhole, playing a game of chess with a colleague. When he saw her, he quickly stubbed out his cigarette in the overflowing ashtray.

'Looks like it, eh? I'm not gonna let the ol' bugger here go without getting me revenge,' he muttered, pointing his stubbly chin at his opponent. 'This is ol' Benno, I don't think you've been introduced. Benno – Frau Peters.'

Lena gave Benno a brief nod before she turned back to Charlie. 'I'm looking for a file, but could only find an empty cover.'

'And what file's that, ma'am?'

'The last case files of Dr Dobelli.'

The second she uttered the name, something changed in Charlie's expression.

'If it ain't on the shelf, I got no idea where it is,' he muttered, and exchanged a glance with Benno before he returned his focus to the game.

'You're quite sure?' Lena asked. She stepped closer, her hands on the table, and leaned over the chessboard to catch Charlie's eye.

Without looking up, he nodded and tapped his index finger pensively on the rook.

'Just an idea,' remarked Lena, running her eyes over the board. 'Move the bishop, then you'll put the king in check, and then in the next go you can take the queen without losing your knight.'

He looked up in surprise then looked back at the board, as if he was going through the moves in his head. Then he whistled softly through his teeth. 'Eh, not bad . . .'

'Hey, that's hardly fair,' grumbled Benno.

'Rubbish! I'd ha' noticed myself in a second.'

Lena grinned and walked off.

'Oh, Frau Peters?'

She stopped.

'Wi' regards to your file, why don't you come ba' tomorrow afternoon? I'll see wha' I can do by then . . .'

Lena gave him a grateful smile and went on her way.

11

When she rode home on her Vespa a short while later, she had a bad feeling in her stomach. On the one hand she could not get Dr Dobelli's missing file out of her head. And she was still furious with Drescher for having failed to mention her predecessor. Lena resented secretiveness. And then there was Christine Wagenbach's grisly account, which remained on her mind long after she had left work. Lena knew that exercise was the only thing that would help. She had to work it off somehow, if she wanted to avoid spending half the night lying awake worrying.

By the time she parked her Vespa in the courtyard of her apartment, it was pouring with rain.

Today is definitely a gym day, Lena thought. So she decided to try out the fitness studio she had read about on the department bulletin board.

12

Lena feared the gym would be heaving, but was pleasantly surprised to find it empty when she arrived half an hour later. She left her bag in a locker before walking into the gym in black leggings and a dark blue top ready to warm up with some stretching. She began her workout with chin-ups then moved onto free weights to work on her arm and shoulder strength.

'You need to stretch your back a bit more,' commented a passing employee in a tracksuit of the same bright blue as the logo of the gym.

Lena gave him a forced smile and nodded.

'I'll be over there if you need a hand, OK?'

'Thanks, but I'm fine.' The last thing she wanted after a day like today was an over-enthusiastic personal trainer hovering around, tirelessly cheering her on.

After a while she put the weights down and walked over to the water cooler.

'Peters.'

Lena turned around. It was Volker Drescher, with a squash bag on his shoulder.

'Herr Drescher . . .' This was the all that she needed.

He grinned. 'No jogging today?'

'No, I thought a change wouldn't hurt, and I saw the notice on the bulletin board about Homicide staff getting half price . . .'

'Then I'll probably see you here quite a lot in the near future,' he said.

Lena managed a polite smile. *I don't suppose that can be avoided.*

'Can I challenge you to a game of squash?' suggested Drescher. 'My friend's just let me down.'

'If you don't mind losing.'

'What? We'll see about that!' he replied jokingly, handing her a racket from his bag. 'Come on then!'

They walked over to the squash court. Drescher threw her the ball with a wink. 'Ladies first.'

Lena took a deep breath in and out, reached up to serve and opened the match. Seeing the power with which she hit the ball quickly wiped the smile off Drescher's face. He had to run to get any chance of hitting the ball. Lena sent the balls crashing across the court and had Drescher running left and right, the rubber soles of his trainers squeaking on the floor. Lena dominated the match. Not only was she fast, she was also more agile than Drescher and she thrashed the ball like she was possessed, the sweat dripping from her forehead. After another intense exchange of volleys, Drescher let the ball go out and turned to Lena, gasping for air.

'My God, you don't half sock it one! Are you trying to kill me?'

Her face bright red, Lena dropped to her knees to catch her breath.

'The case seems to really be getting to you . . .' said Drescher, with difficulty.

She stood up and ran her sweatband over her damp forehead, without taking her eyes off Drescher. 'That's not it.'

'What then?'

Lena looked him straight in the eye. 'Why didn't you tell me that you'd already had a profiler on the case?'

Drescher looked away. He picked his towel up from the bench and wiped his sweaty neck. 'I saw no reason for it.'

'No reason? You want me to produce a comprehensive offender profile and saw no reason to tell me?' Lena's eyes widened in anger. 'Dr Dobelli's case file should have been waiting for me on my desk!'

He shrugged. 'After Dobelli threw in the towel, I thought it best if you were completely impartial when you started on the case. Surely you understand that? But if the file is so important to you, why don't you just fetch it from the archive?'

'Because it's not there!'

Drescher looked at her, surprised. 'That's odd . . . very strange.'

Lena looked at him sharply. She doubted his surprise was genuine. Nevertheless, there was no point going on about it. If she really wanted to know what had happened to her predecessor, she would have to take the matter into her own hands.

'I'll see you tomorrow,' she said tersely, leaving the racket on the bench and taking her towel with her as she left the squash court.

13

It was already late in the evening by the time Lena got home. She fed the cat, sat in front of the TV and ate a cheese baguette that she had bought, along with a bottle of Merlot, from the little bistro around the corner on the way back from the gym. Bored, she flicked through the channels but, finding only game shows and reality TV, she turned it off again and took what was left of her baguette back into the kitchen. Lena uncorked the red wine, poured herself a glass and took it to the bathroom. She lit a few candles and got undressed. With a sigh, she climbed into the comforting water.

Perfect: exactly what I needed. She closed her eyes and felt her limbs gradually relax as she mentally reviewed her eventful first day at the Berlin homicide division. She thought about her new office and the many new faces she still needed to get to know. Rebecca Brandt, who seemed a little forward, but was basically fine. Volker Drescher, who she hadn't quite got to the bottom of yet. And Ben Vogt, the redhead, who gave the impression that he was afraid she might threaten his rank. But with a little luck the next few weeks would probably not be half as bad as she had feared, at least as far as working with Brandt was concerned. She picked up her glass of red wine, which she had placed on the edge of the bath. Lena took a large sip and felt the wine flow down her throat and calm her nerves. Lena put the wine glass down on the edge of the bath and leaned back into the water. Involuntarily, her thoughts returned to Christine Wagenbach. Lena felt her guilty conscience about the interview gnaw at her and, in hindsight, was annoyed for being forced to follow Drescher's orders against her own will. Nevertheless, she had to admit that the conversation had been insightful and Drescher's ruthless approach had been justified.

Lena was lying back with the water up to her neck when she heard a strange scratching coming from the hallway. She opened her eyes, sat up and listened. *What was that?* And there it was again suddenly. A faint scratching. She quickly stood up, grabbed a towel and stepped out of the bath. She wrapped herself in the towel and walked into the unlit hallway. Water dripped from her wet hair onto the floorboards. In the moonlight that fell in through the window, she recognised Napoleon. The cat licked his front paw before he mewed, startled by something, and slipped behind one of the cardboard boxes. Lena tiptoed along, nervously looking around. She felt a light breeze brush against her. She froze, as if struck by lightning, when she saw that the apartment door was ajar. She stood there in the hallway, motionless for a second, feeling her pulse racing. She was sure that the door had caught the latch as she closed it, when she'd come in with the wine and baguette. The wooden floor creaked beneath her feet as she slowly walked towards the door, placed her hand on the handle and opened it a fraction more. She scanned the dark courtyard outside. Not a sound. Lena went back inside. She closed the door and double-locked it. But there was that sound again. The scratching came from within her apartment. Very slowly, Lena turned around. Someone was in her bedroom!

Without turning on the light, she hurried to the kitchen. She fumbled with sweaty palms along the work surface for the large bread knife, found it and crept straight back to the bedroom. At the threshold, she paused. Then she realised what was making that noise. It was nothing more than a branch brushing in the wind against the patio door, which was ajar. Lena had to laugh at herself as she put down the knife. She pulled the door to, then rubbed her temples. Was the case getting to her more than she cared to admit? She decided to get into her pyjamas, have another glass of wine and then go straight to bed.

She placed the knife under the mattress just in case.

14

Early hours of Tuesday morning, 10th May

Lena spent the whole night tossing and turning while the faces of the murdered women kept resurfacing in her mind. She wondered how long it would be before the 'Mutilator', as the tabloids now called the culprit, was convicted.

How many innocent women will you kill before I find you?

She finally admitted defeat about four hours before sunrise. She simply couldn't get the case out of her head. She got out of bed, put on her dressing gown and went into the study to struggle through her tomes on psychology and psychiatry. Lena could recite the contents of these books in her sleep, but she still thought that perhaps she might come across an idea or an approach that she had not yet thought of.

A while later, Lena rubbed her eyes. She propped her elbows on the desk and flipped through her notebook, deep in thought. She turned to look out at the darkness through the window, then switched on her laptop and began to type.

The perpetrator's actions are highly calculated, cold and merciless. Focussed exclusively on his mission, he feels no empathy towards his victims, let alone guilt. This is supported by the fact that the interval between the murders is getting shorter. That he is a sadist is clear not only from the fact that he injects his victims with alcuronium chloride, but also that he leaves them to their fate, rather than killing them after the amputation. But why does he leave himself vulnerable to the risk that the victim could survive? As happened with Christine Wagenbach. Is it an absolute lack of emotion or simply deep-rooted hatred? He is intelligent enough to approach his victims without arousing suspicion. Christine Wagenbach confirmed that the perpetrator was male and strong to overpower his victims.

It is possible that the perpetrator is not necessarily physically stronger, but has a well-developed knack for manipulating his victims, enabling him to successfully wield control over them. On top of that he behaves in an inconspicuous manner, probably leading an outwardly conventional life even if it might be fair to assume that he is not masquerading as a loving father. Because he has not sexually abused any of his victims, it is conceivable that he is either gay or asexual. He focusses solely on his plan and feels neither desire nor lust. This makes him all the more unpredictable. But what is the delusional ideology which underlies his behaviour? A motivation for such acts is often a destabilising factor, such as a traumatic event. But how does that fit with how he chooses his victims, who could hardly be more different?

Gazing out of the window, Lena again went over what Wagenbach had told her in hospital. She pieced together every little detail like a jigsaw, not resting until she was satisfied with the psychological portrait she had constructed.

15

When Lena walked into the meeting room at nine on the dot, the members of the special commission team were already gathered there. Volker Drescher had had to excuse himself because of an urgent appointment and had left a message for Lena that she could start without him.

'Good morning all,' said Lena. She hung up her charcoal grey trench coat and, wearing jeans and a dark jacket, her hair scraped back into a severe ponytail, she stepped to the front to address her colleagues. She was somewhat nervous, exacerbated by her sense that something about the meeting was 'off'. She stood in front of the wall covered in photos of the mutilated women and waited until the police officers had sat down.

'This morning I'm going to share with you my thoughts about the psyche of our perpetrator and bring you up to date with the investigation. As you know, Frau Brandt and I were at the hospital yesterday with Christine Wagenbach,' she began as she heard a whisper here and there. Trying to mask her uncertainty, she opened her notebook and summarised the main points of Wagenbach's account.

'With regards to both the mutilation and murder, every compulsive offender follows a recurring pattern of behaviour, his own ritual, which has to be followed with, for example, an unchanging sequence of violence – that's the only way he can hope to obtain the satisfaction he craves,' Lena continued. As her eyes passed over the increasingly restive audience, she noticed how Ben Vogt, who had sat next to her at the meeting the previous day, whispered something to Rebecca Brandt. Suddenly Brandt gave Lena a strange look and gestured with her index finger cutting across her throat, as if to give Lena a signal. Lena had no idea what she meant and carried on outlining her profile of the perpetrator without wavering.

Suddenly Volker Drescher entered the room. As Vogt noticed him, he loudly cleared his throat, as if to raise an objection.

'Just a moment, please,' asked Lena. 'I'm nearly done. With regards to Wagenbach, I'm going to go back to the hospital and, besides a description of the perpetrator, I hope to get one or two clues about the potential next victim from her.' Sighing, she ran her hand through her hair. 'But to be honest, I'm not too optimistic about our chances: the young woman will be too traumatised to make any kind of reliable prediction. Nevertheless, at the moment, she's our only hope. She also said that she heard his voice. Although it was only a faint mumble, she thinks she would recognise it. Christine Wagenbach also mentioned having heard music. This appears to have been opera. To my shame I must confess that I can count the number of times I've been to the opera on one hand.' She looked over at Lucy Gittinger. 'Lucy, I gather you go to the opera quite often. I would like you to come to the hospital with me to help work out which opera it was.'

'Um, Frau Peters . . .' stammered Lucy before she looked over to Drescher for support.

'Christine Wagenbach died last night at the hospital,' Drescher said, before clearing his throat and straightening his glasses. 'Her heart stopped at around four in the morning. All attempts to revive her failed. There was nothing the doctors could do for her.'

Lena felt as if he had slapped her in the face. She took a deep breath. 'And this is the first I'm told?' She struggled to maintain her composure.

'I assumed Hen Vogt would have already informed you,' said Drescher, giving Ben Vogt a disapproving look.

Lena could hear the swoosh of blood in her ears. 'Yes, that would have been appropriate!' Stunned, she looked alternately at Drescher and the redheaded Vogt. *What were they thinking, keeping this from me?*

'Sorry, but no one told me that I should tell her,' Vogt said.

Lena felt her mouth go dry. If Christine Wagenbach had died because of her, she would never forgive herself.

'I want you to know that Wagenbach's death was completely unrelated to her nervous breakdown during your interview with her at the hospital,' stated Drescher, turning to Lena as if reading her thoughts. 'Wagenbach died of septicaemia as a result of the amputation.'

Lena nodded in a daze. But the hoped-for sense of relief did not come. Refusing to look either Vogt or Drescher in the eye, she left the meeting room.

16

Lena stormed down the corridor with long strides. *He actually let me stand there like an idiot!* She closed the door to the Ladies' behind her, rushed to the sink and washed her hands several times. Again and again she pressed the soap dispenser, washing and rinsing her hands. Only after a while, when her fingers were red from rubbing, did she manage to turn off the water and pause for a moment.

Calm down, damn it! She leaned against the sink and closed her eyes for a second. Then she reached for the paper towel dispenser.

'Come on, you bastard thing!' she hissed, trying to pull a piece out. But the dispenser was defiant. Lena was wildly yanking at it when she saw Rebecca Brandt in the mirror.

'You want to rip the thing off the wall?'

Lena dropped her wet hands by her side.

'I'm sorry about how that went,' said Brandt. 'I thought you already knew that Wagenbach was dead . . .'

Lena shook her head. 'First Drescher kept me in the dark about my predecessor disappearing – just like her file – and now this.'

'He really shouldn't have let you carry on in front of the whole team like that,' Brandt agreed. 'Yeah, the carrot and the stick – that's his way when he finds someone good . . .' she said, half joking.

'Good? Don't make me laugh!' Lena shook her head again and wiped her hands on her jeans. 'Oh well,' she sighed after she had composed herself a little. 'It's not important.' A lie.

Rebecca Brandt gave her a sympathetic look, then disappeared into a toilet cubicle. 'At lunchtime we're going to the sandwich shop on the corner,' she called from the cubicle. 'Want to come too?'

Lena leaned over the tap and had a sip of water. She wiped her mouth with the back of her hand and said, 'Thanks, but I've got a lot to do.' Lena knew it was an offer of reconciliation, but she needed to make some progress on the case and prove herself. Especially after that embarrassing scene. She also wanted to use the opportunity to pay another visit to the archives to track down Dr Dobelli's case file. After that she wanted to stop by Dr Kurt Böttner in Pathology to ask him personally about anything he might have noticed or anything the victims had in common. Maybe there was some tiny detail that was not mentioned in the autopsy report and that had not been taken into consideration thus far.

'You're sure?' she heard Rebecca Brandt ask.

'Thank you, I appreciate it. But I'll see you later,' Lena called to her, already at the door. She wanted to go to her office now and get on with work.

As she stepped out, she saw Volker Drescher disappear into the men's toilets next door.

17

A few hours later

Her feet crossed on the desk, Lena looked out of the window, down onto the car park, thinking hard. Three hours had passed since her embarrassing presentation at the team meeting and she was no further forwards. Her visit to Charlie in the archives had been unsuccessful. Despite extensive searches, he had been unable to find either Dr Dobelli's case notes nor any copies of them. And Lena's detour to Pathology brought no new insight.

The knock on the door shook her out of her thoughts.

Lena took her feet off the desk and sat up. 'Come in.'

It was Rebecca Brandt, who had just come back from her lunch break. She stepped into the office and put a tuna sandwich on the desk in front of Lena.

'Here, or you'll waste away.'

Lena looked down at the sandwich. 'Thank you,' she said, smiling. 'You didn't need to.' A blatant lie. Her stomach had been growling for ages; she was ravenous. Half resting on the desk, Brandt leaned over towards Lena.

'You didn't hear this from me, but with regards to Dobelli's case file –' She threw a quick glance over her shoulder at the open door before she carried on, 'I think I saw Drescher put it in his desk drawer.'

Lena crossed her arms over her chest and looked at her with a frown. 'Is that right? Interesting.'

She and Charlie might have been searching for some time. 'Thanks,' she said, smiling.

'Don't mention it,' Brandt replied.

As soon as she had left the office, Lena fell upon the sandwich. She wolfed it down and was still eating when the phone on her desk rang.

'Peters,' Lena answered, her mouth full.

It was Volker Drescher. 'Listen, Peters, Ferdinand Roggendorf has a country house in Brandenburg. Underwear belonging to the maths student has been found and taken in.'

Lena put down the rest of the sandwich and wiped her mouth with a napkin as she listened to the rest of Drescher's report.

'Roggendorf is already at the station. Ben Vogt is just about to question him.'

With the handset in her hand, Lena jumped up. 'OK. I'll be right there.'

18

'Roggendorf claims not to have the slightest idea how Novak's knickers and bra ended up at his country house,' said Drescher, striding along the corridor to the interrogation room as Lena followed a few paces behind.

'He also denies that the girl has ever been there,' he continued.

'You said there was a neighbour who said she heard screams from the house. Did she ever see Yvonne Novak go in or out?' Lena inquired.

Drescher shook his head. 'Apparently not. But the DNA test confirms that the underwear is definitely Yvonne Novak's.'

'Has anything else been found?'

'Forensics have found all kinds of crosses, pendulums, tarot cards and stuff related to the occult. There was animal blood smeared all over the walls and pentagons scratched into the walls. And about a dozen vials of a chloride substance have been taken in.'

Lena looked at him quizzically. 'Alcuronium chloride?'

'Still to be confirmed. But apart from the underwear, so far we've got nothing we can nail him with – a few vials of chemicals are not enough to prove he's the killer of Yvonne Novak, let alone the other women.' He held the door open to Lena to the tiny cupboard-like room with a tinted-glass window looking onto the interrogation room next door. 'Oh, Peters . . .'

'Yes?'

'Nice blouse.' He winked at her.

Lena raised her eyebrows. 'Thanks,' she replied, somewhat bemused by his inappropriate remark. She stepped over to the tinted glass and watched with her arms crossed as Ferdinand Roggendorf was interrogated by Ben Vogt. Roggendorf was not particularly tall and was dressed in a rather extravagant fashion. He was wearing eyeliner and his dark brown hair was held firmly in place with great quantities of hair gel. With his embroidered velvet jacket, tight-fitting leather trousers, knee-high boots studded with rivets and thin moustache, he seemed to Lena more like a poor imitation of Prince than what she might have expected of the son of a senior barrister. Roggendorf sat casually in his chair, his legs spread out and one arm resting on the chair back. His posture suggested calm self-confidence, but Lena didn't buy it: it seemed a little contrived to her eyes. With his left hand he placed a cigarette between his thin lips.

'No smoking in here,' remarked Vogt, tearing the cigarette from Roggendorf's mouth with a jerky motion, shaking Lena from her thoughts.

Ferdinand Roggendorf groaned with annoyance and stroked his moustache. 'Listen, I've told you everything I know. And I know my rights –' he pointed a finger at the police officer – 'so unless you have something specific to talk about, you're lucky that I'm even here. So, a little more respect, if you don't mind?'

Lena raised her eyebrows and looked at Drescher, who stood next to her at the tinted glass. He took off his glasses and looked back at her.

'Peters, are you ready?' he asked, with a nod towards the interrogation room.

'Sure,' Lena said.

'OK, let's see what you've got,' said Drescher. He went over to the desk, pressed a button and spoke through the microphone into the interrogation room.

'We'll take a short break.'

No sooner had Drescher's voice rung out than Lena saw Ben Vogt's face turn sour and his lower jaw drop. He bent to pick up his notes, then left the room. When she met him in the doorway, his displeasure at her taking over the interrogation was written on his face. She gave him a fleeting smile before closing the door to the interrogation room behind her. She had to be on her guard in front of Vogt. His petty jealousy was the last thing she needed right now.

Lena sat down opposite Ferdinand Roggendorf. A bitter, expensive-smelling men's fragrance tickled her nose.

'My name's Lena Peters. I'm a criminal psychologist and I'd like to ask you a few questions.' She put her notebook down on the Formica tabletop. 'Should I address you as "Herr Roggendorf" or use your screen name "Dark Armon"?'

His cheek muscles twitched and there was something mischievous in his expression. 'You can call me what you like,' he said, leaning forwards slightly. 'But I haven't got all day. Not even for you, Miss Criminal Psychologist.'

Lena pursed her lips. 'If you prefer, I can happily bring my colleague back in again.'

He scowled at her. 'Nah, stay. But I still don't understand what all this is about.' He shrugged his shoulders and shook his head. 'I'm being treated like a fucking criminal!'

Lena raised one corner of her mouth. 'You're quite right.' She pushed back her chair and went over to the door.

'Could we have some coffee please?' she called out into the corridor.

Roggendorf smiled. 'Black, please, with sugar.'

'Black with sugar!' Lena relayed.

Shortly afterwards, Lucy brought in a tray with one cup of coffee and a bowl of sugar.

'Thank you, Lucy,' said Lena as Lucy left the room.

Roggendorf opened his eyes wide and grinned at Lena. 'You haven't been here long, huh?'

She shook her head without taking her eyes off him.

His grin broadened as he sank two sugar cubes into his coffee. 'It shows.'

Lena watched him as he stirred his coffee, quietly scrutinising him. Roggendorf was very well groomed and clearly paid a lot of attention to his appearance. The only thing out of place was the slight trace of oil on the cuffs of his grey silk skirt, which an inattentive observer would probably never notice. *Could the oil marks be from the junkyard, where Novak's body was found?* Lena decided to begin the interrogation.

'What was your relationship with Yvonne Novak?'

His grin vanished abruptly. 'We were vaguely acquainted.' He put his cup to his mouth. As he did, the cuff of his shirt slid down and revealed a tattoo. As Roggendorf noticed Lena's glance, he quickly pulled his cuff back to cover it.

Frowning, Lena looked up. 'So you weren't particularly close?'

He breathed out with a whistle. 'OK, I'll say this again very slowly so you can write it down: I have no idea how Yvonne Novak got into my country house, if that's what you're getting at. And I've had nothing to do with her underwear. Yvonne was a casual acquaintance from the chatroom, nothing more.' He grinned again. 'But if you so desperately want to foist some dirty knickers on me, you can give me yours if you like . . .'

Lena did not react. It didn't even occur to her to respond to his provocation. 'And what about Christine Wagenbach, Rea Schmidt, Laura Höllberg, Petra Lorenz, Sandra Köstner and all the other women? Were they also just *casual* acquaintances?'

Roggendorf looked at her over the rim of his coffee cup and suddenly looked tenser. Lena closed her notebook and took out some pictures of the victims she had mentioned. All the photos were taken post mortem. She shoved them across the table.

Roggendorf sat quite still for a moment, letting his gaze wander over the photos. 'I don't know what you want from me. I've never seen these women before,' he said with a terse shrug and put down his coffee cup.

Lena put another photo on the table in front of him. 'This is Yvonne Novak,' she said, tapping her finger on the image.

'I can see that!' he snapped, and for the first time there was something else in his expression. Something that Lena could not quite put her finger on. But just as she had that feeling, the door opened and a bloated red-cheeked man in a tailored suit burst into the interrogation room.

Dr Richard Roggendorf. Lena knew his face from a number of talk shows. *Shit!*

'Ferdinand, we're leaving! You've got nothing to talk to these people about!'

The young Roggendorf stood up and gave Lena a dirty grin. 'See you again, perhaps,' he said quietly, winking at her as he left the room.

Lena sat there without moving for a moment before following him out and watching as he trotted along behind his father, who stamped along the corridor.

19

'Great. This is guaranteed not to be the last we hear of it,' muttered Ben Vogt, who came back into the interrogation room with Volker Drescher.

As if he had heard him, Richard Roggendorf turned to throw him a warning glare. 'You watch it, Drescher!' he shouted down the hallway. 'I know your lot never have a search warrant!' Then he shoved open the door out to the car park.

Drescher brushed his threat off with a shake of his head, while the three of them stood in the corridor watching as the lawyer and his son disappeared outside.

'So, what do you think of Ferdinand Roggendorf?' Drescher asked, turning to Lena.

'Well, if you ask me, the guy has definitely got a skeleton in the closet,' said Ben Vogt.

'I asked Frau Peters.'

Vogt huffed. Drescher took a deep breath, but made no effort to rebuke him. He and Lena walked down the hall, and without another word, Vogt tagged along after them.

'Ferdinand Roggendorf drank his coffee with his right hand,' Lena began.

'So what?' interrupted Vogt. 'What's that got to do with the case?'

'Everything. Our culprit is most likely left-handed, right?' Lena ascertained.

Drescher nodded at her. 'Correct.'

'Could be a coincidence,' Vogt countered.

Lena looked over her shoulder at him. 'As far as I know you're also left-handed – at least during meetings I've seen you write with your left hand.'

'Yes, and . . . ?'

'And if I remember correctly, you type text messages with your left thumb.' She paused. 'Can you honestly imagine doing it with your right thumb?'

Vogt pulled a face. 'What? Uh, no . . .'

'You see,' said Lena.

'But what about those vials he has stashed away?' asked Vogt. 'I mean, shit, that was enough to inject a whole army!'

Drescher looked at him, frowning. 'It still isn't enough to pin a murder on him. At most we could get him for theft.'

Vogt narrowed his eyes.

'Roggendorf has a tattoo on his forearm,' Lena added as they carried on walking. 'It looked like it might have been some occult symbols.'

Still walking, Drescher gave her a nod of recognition and exchanged a glance with Vogt.

'Maybe the symbols have some link with the victims,' suggested Vogt.

Lena shook her head. 'That would seem too simplistic to me.' She screwed her eyes up thoughtfully. 'We should still look into it . . .'

'And what do you think Roggendorf will do next?' asked Drescher.

She stopped in front of the door to her office. 'If he is in fact our man, then for the time being he'll lie low . . .'

'That's the case solved,' said Vogt.

Lena looked at both Vogt and Drescher. 'Essentially, I'd say we should be careful about drawing any conclusions, especially when it comes to Roggendorf,' she stressed, before looking at Ben Vogt again. 'Have you already confirmed whether any of the other women besides Yvonne Novak used this chatroom – the one where she met Roggendorf?'

Vogt shook his head and shrugged. 'There's no evidence that they did.'

Lena nodded and chewed on her lower lip. 'Thanks anyway,' she said and added, 'Oh and Ben, would you please find out what the symbols tattooed on his arm are? Thank you.'

'How do you mean?'

Lena looked at him. 'Give Roggendorf a visit or think of a way to get close to him,' she said and, without waiting for him to agree, she gave him and Drescher a polite smile. 'If you'll excuse me, I'd better get on.' She went back into her office.

As soon as she had closed the door behind her, Lena leaned against it and exhaled. She had her first interrogation of the case behind her; whether or not it was successful remained to be seen. Ferdinand Roggendorf was playing a game with them, that much was certain. He was smart enough to know that he did not need to come to the station without an official legal summons. And yet he did agree to come in. Lena went to the window and looked out at the car park.

Ferdinand Roggendorf was an arrogant young man who clearly got a kick out of testing his limits – but was he really capable of murder?

20

Afternoon press conference at the Ritz-Carlton Hotel

Once his old acquaintance in the security team had sneaked him through the security checkpoint and given him access to the already overcrowded press room, the man who called himself Artifex stood amid the bustle of journalists and photographers and looked around for the petite reporter. Where was she then? Where was she hiding? He scratched nervously at his neck, grabbed a press pack for Jeffrey Maloney's new film from the table and strolled through the crowd keeping his eyes peeled for her, until he finally saw her sitting near the front of the auditorium. She had her hair pinned up this time and she was wearing pearl earrings and a white blouse that would have lent her an innocent look, were it not unbuttoned so low. With this she wore a knee-length pinstripe skirt and high heels, as if she feared being overlooked because of her height. And as if fate had willed it to be, the space beside her was still free. Artifex smoothed back his blond wavy hair and strode purposefully towards her before anyone else could occupy the seat.

'Is this seat free?' he asked with his most charming smile.

The reporter looked up. 'Sure,' she said, before going back to looking around excitedly for her beloved movie star. When everyone was seated and the doors to the hall were closed, Jeffrey Maloney appeared and, together with his entourage, he took a seat on the podium, behind which hung a huge poster for the new blockbuster.

This Maloney, whose nose was as flat as his acting, did not look half as good as on the big screen, Artifex thought derisively. But he seemed to make a powerful impression on the petite reporter. Artifex glanced discreetly at her lips, which were opening ever wider the longer she stared at the American movie star. *My God, they're perfect!* He could still hardly believe his luck. His eyes darted over the laminated ID pass pinned to her blouse where it was easy to see. *Svenja Stollberg, Star Biz editorial*, Artifex read. A pretty name. Tilla would definitely like it.

He forced himself to look straight ahead again.

What followed were the standard questions from the press, and Maloney answered the more challenging questions – in so far as there were any – only after consultation with his management. Maloney's every word, his slightest gesture, was captured by these journos, industriously scribbling away. True to form, Artifex also pulled out a notepad and raised his hand to ask Maloney a question. When it was finally his turn to ask, Artifex leaned back in his chair and, for a moment, scrutinised the clean-shaven man in the cream-coloured shirt and the tacky gold chain, before he asked in English whether he was really acting in front of the camera or if he was also an actor in real life every now and then. As predicted, Maloney did not see the irony in his question and spouted nothing but drivel in response. But that did not bother Artifex; all he intended was to make an impression on the petite reporter, who was herself too excited and nervous to ask a question.

And indeed she gave Artifex a fleeting smile before turning her attention back to Mr Superstar.

'Oh damn,' groaned Artifex, as he reached a hand inside his jacket pocket. 'Looks like I've left my pen at the office . . .'

'Here, I have a spare,' whispered Svenja Stollberg and reached for a pen for him from her handbag. A quick glance at the parking ticket lying in the handbag confirmed to Artifex that Svenja Stollberg had indeed come by car.

'Thank you, you're a lifesaver,' he replied, giving her a wink as he took the pen.

She had taken the bait.

21

Svenja Stollberg was quick to leave the hall when the press conference finished, in a rush to type up her impressions of 'the Big Maloney' before the copy deadline.

Night night, time for beddy-byes, thought Artifex as he followed the petite reporter through the foyer with a grin. Taking cover in the crowd, he stayed close behind her as they both crossed the street outside the hotel, while the young woman walked to the car park with her mobile to her ear, apparently unable to avoid involving the entire outside world in her excited chatter about what she'd just experienced. She therefore did not notice that Artifex had split away from the crowd and was hurrying into the four-storey car park behind her. He pulled out a cap and pulled it down low over his face. The next thing he saw was Svenja Stollberg disappearing into one of the lifts. Artifex stopped and watched the display show which floor it was on. He stepped into the lift when it came and waited for the doors to close. *Come on, let's go!* He shifted his weight impatiently from one foot to the other.

When the doors opened a few moments later, he saw the young woman walking briskly to her car. Artifex looked around for CCTV cameras. He was lucky that Stollberg had parked her silver grey Lupo behind a pillar, which blocked the view of the driver's seat. Artifex followed her through the car park and waited until Stollberg had finished her call, put her phone back in her bag and got in behind the wheel, before he said anything.

'Hi, excuse me!' he shouted and came striding towards her car. 'Your pen – I forgot to give it back!'

The young woman opened the window and looked incredulously at him. 'But you could have kept it . . .'

Artifex rested one hand on the roof of the Lupo as he leaned down and smiled at her. 'Oh no, I couldn't.' With his left hand, he held the pen out to her through the open car window, holding it in such a way that the needle of the syringe was concealed under his wrist. As soon as she took the pen, he would stab her. As the anaesthetic would act within seconds, the danger that Svenja Stollberg would attract any attention was relatively low.

'No, really – it's OK,' the reporter insisted.

Artifex's smile was now so wide it almost hurt his cheek muscles. 'But I insist on giving it back. Honestly, take it . . .'

The instant that the reporter went to reach for the pen, a deep voice rang out behind them: 'Hey, Svenja! Will you give me a lift back to the office?'

To Artifex's immense irritation, a lanky guy with an SLR in his hand came loping in their direction. Artifex quickly retracted his hand and hid the pen and syringe away in his jacket pocket.

Damn it! he cursed, forcing himself to maintain his composure. Once again it occurred to him how helpful it would be in situations like this to have a partner with him. Someone like Gemmy, he thought briefly before dismissing the idea again.

'See you around,' he said quickly, and he gave Svenja Stollberg a brief nod then disappeared before the press photographer reached the car.

When, a few moments later, the reporter drove her Lupo out of the car park with the paparazzo in the passenger seat, Artifex stood behind a pillar and noted down the licence plate.

Don't worry, Tilla – she won't get away . . . I'll get her sooner or later. And he already had an idea of how he would contrive it.

22

It was nearly 10 o'clock when Lena pushed aside the stack of documents relating to the case and yawned, stretching her arms out above her head. She stood up and opened the window a little to let in some fresh air. It was dark outside and, again, she was the last one to leave the station. At least so she thought – until she looked down at the parking lot and realised she was not.

Strange – I thought they were long gone, she mused as she spotted Volker Drescher and Rebecca Brandt in the light of the street-lamp, walking together to their cars. Lena could hardly believe her eyes when she then saw her boss and Brandt exchange an intimate farewell kiss. Lena gasped and quickly switched off the light to avoid being spotted. She went back over to the window and peered out at the car park, surprised and amused in equal measure.

So is Drescher an improvement on Brandt's property shark? Volker Drescher clearly has a lot more secrets than I imagined, thought Lena, as Dr Cornelia Dobelli's case notes again came to mind. She considered it for a moment after Drescher and Brandt set off in opposite directions. After a brief hesitation, she eventually crept along the unlit corridor to Drescher's office.

She was well aware that what she was doing constituted a breach of protocol, and yet she saw it as inevitable. The doors to the other offices were open. Here and there was the faint glow of a screen on standby or the flicker of a monitor. Otherwise, everything was dark. Although she was convinced she was doing the right thing, Lena still felt like she was breaking and entering. The door to Drescher's office gave an ominous creak as Lena entered the room. It was much more spacious than the other offices. There was a golf bag in the corner and in front of the window there was a massage table. Lena turned on the lamp on the broad mahogany desk, which had several pens and a stack of Drescher's signed books on it. Then she carefully pulled open the top drawer. Among paperclips, pencils, cigars and framed photos of his two grown sons, Lena found a copy of her CV and an old edition of *The Criminologist*. It was the edition from a few months ago in which Lena had published a report on new approaches to operational case analysis. Drescher had bookmarked the relevant page with a yellow Post-it note. The photograph of Lena printed with the article was circled with red pen. Without quite knowing what to make of that, Lena put the magazine back, and suddenly the door to the office was pushed open. The ceiling light went on. Startled, Lena turned around.

'Frau Wang – you made me jump!' she exclaimed with relief as she recognised the cleaning lady, who she had met the night before.

Wang gave her a friendly nod. 'Good evening, Frau Peters. You the last in the office again.'

Lena smiled and watched as the woman pushed her cleaning trolley down the corridor. Then she opened the next drawer down, looking through its contents carefully, not rummaging, before she finally found what she was looking for tucked between two folders: Dr Cornelia Dobelli's investigation files. Lena flipped through the collection of notes, sketches and crime scene photos. But as far as she could tell, there was nothing that hinted at a cause for Dr Dobelli's disappearance. Absorbed in thought, Lena looked up. She had the sensation that she was not alone in the room. There were firm footsteps approaching, which she was sure were not those of Ms Wang.

23

'Can I help you?'

Lena froze for a second before she slowly turned to face Drescher.

'For God's sake – what are you doing here?'

Lena began to stammer. 'I . . . I . .' *Shit!*

'Are you out of your mind?' he snapped and snatched Dr Dobelli's file.

Lena stood up. It was about time *he* finally explained himself. 'What is Dr Dobelli's case file doing in your desk?'

'I have no idea,' he replied angrily as he glared fiercely at her over his glasses. 'But what I do know is that you have gone too far!' He pointed his finger at Lena, his eyes blazing. 'You know that I consider you an excellent profiler – but apparently you have forgotten who is in charge of the investigation here!'

Lena threw up her hands. 'OK, OK – I've screwed up,' she admitted, more to gain time than anything.

'You have abused my trust!'

'But—' she began.

'No buts, Peters – that's it, you're out of here!'

Speechless, Lena studied his face. 'You're taking me off the case?' The atmosphere in the room was so tense it could snap.

'That's right. And now get out of my office,' he ordered, pointing a finger at the door.

Lena felt both hot and cold at the same time. 'I don't believe it! First you absolutely must have me on the case and now you're throwing me out?'

He sat down at his desk, indicating the conversation was over as far as he was concerned.

Screw you, Drescher!

'Fine, as you wish. I'm going.' Her knees felt wobbly as Lena hurried back to her office with tears of rage in her eyes and grabbed her possessions as quickly as she could. Drescher was still sitting behind his desk with the door open when she walked past carrying her box of things and he did not honour her with so much as a look. As Lena headed past the vacant offices towards the exit, she could almost hear the chatter of the police officers who had been waiting for her to slip up.

24

Potsdamer Platz was swarming with people. Black limousines were parked outside the back entrance to the cinema, and amid the camera crews, paparazzi and journalists crowded around the red carpet were excited fans who broke into screams when Jeffrey Maloney and the rest of the cast made their appearance.

Artifex was observing the events from a distance. The good thing about events like this film premiere was that a nobody like him, a stranger in the crowd, did not draw any attention. In his blue jeans and jacket, he might have been taken for a journalist or an autograph hunter. But certainly not for a human hunter.

He still had not seen his petite reporter, but he was pretty sure that she would be at this exclusive screening for celebrities and members of the press. She wouldn't have missed it for the world. And so he waited patiently in front of the cinema's press lounge. It would undoubtedly be worth the wait. When he spotted an enthusiastic-looking Svenja Stollberg leaving the cinema foyer two hours later, Artifex calmly popped another salmon canapé in his mouth without taking his eyes off her. She had changed her outfit for the premiere: she was dressed up to the nines. Her skirt was much shorter than the one she had worn at the press conference that afternoon. With it she wore a low-cut chiffon blouse and she had transformed her previously piled-up hair into a wild mane. When he saw that she was heading for the door, he cut across her path with his mobile to the ear.

'OK, got it ... Of course I'm coming – I wouldn't miss a private party with Jeffrey Maloney!' he said into his mobile just loud enough that the petite reporter couldn't fail to catch it.

Stollberg promptly stopped and turned to him with a provocative look. 'Oh, it's the man with no pen,' she said and smiled.

'Not any more, now I have yours,' he said with a grin.

Svenja Stollberg's contrived smile grew broader. 'So you're going to Maloney's private party?'

'Well, yeah.'

'It's here at the hotel, in one of the suites, right?'

He had to smile.

25

'Here?' Artifex laughed scornfully. He stepped towards her until he was less than half a metre away from her and whispered to her behind his hand: 'At least that's the official version. You know, because of the paparazzi and so on.' With a grin on his face he left the cinema at a fast walking pace, knowing that the petite reporter would follow him.

'And unofficially?' she asked, hurrying behind him, clearly intrigued.

Artifex paused. 'Sorry, but I'm not sure if I'm authorised to tell you,' he sighed and continued at a fast pace down the road. He heard the clicking of her heels.

'Wait a minute, will you?' she called and caught up with him again. It was quite clear from her face that she was desperate to know. 'Listen,' she said. She raised her hand as if she were making an oath. 'If you take me with you to the party, I promise on everything I hold sacred not to publish a single word about it. I'm a huge fan of Jeffrey Maloney – I'd do anything for a chance like this.' Now she put on her sweetest little-girl smile again.

Artifex looked around briefly. They had left the hubbub and all the flashing lights of the paparazzi around Potsdamer Platz and now stood just a few metres from his car, which he had parked in a quiet side street.

'Hmm, OK,' he sighed. 'But just so we're clear: this is my story and woe betide you if I see a single line about this party in your rag tomorrow!'

'Party? Which party?' she replied, chuckling.

Artifex nodded and paced ahead. 'Come on, my car's over there.'

'I've got my car too. The best thing is if you wait here – I'll get mine and I'll follow you there.'

'What, so you rock up with your paparazzo friend?!' he snorted indignantly. 'Forget it! Either you come with me, or we'll call it off.'

'All right . . .' groaned Svenja Stollberg, rolling her eyes.

Moments later, she was sitting in the passenger seat of his aging black van, which Tilla used to use to transport all sorts of junk. In between, Artifex used the vehicle for his own transportation purposes.

'So where is this party then?' Svenja Stollberg asked as he was manoeuvring out of the parking space.

'In a hotel near Spandau.' He briefly thought about picking up Gemmy from Jebens Strasse and finally letting him watch as he accomplished a small medical miracle in his workshop. But Artifex knew it was not possible. The risk that he had over-estimated the boy was simply too great. So he abandoned the idea again. He stole a glance now and again at the reporter, who looked out of the window and tapped her manicured nails on the handbag that lay on her lap.

After a while she turned to him and smiled. 'This is really nice of you – I can't tell you how much this means to me.' The excitement was literally written across her face.

And to me, he thought as he turned onto the main road.

'If I can somehow return the favour . . .' she said with a shrug.

Artifex ran his tongue over his lower lip. 'Sure . . .'

She evidently had not envisaged him answering in such a way. Uncertain, she smiled. 'And that would be?'

A strange glint appeared in Artifex's eyes and he glanced fleetingly at her lips. 'You have something that I'd like . . .'

'What? Another pen?' she laughed.

Artifex sucked in through his teeth and shook his head. 'Not quite . . .'

'Then what?'

With a mysterious smile he turned towards Spandau and put his foot on the pedal.

Don't worry, you'll find out soon enough.

26

Late at night in a bar, Friedrichshain, Berlin

Lena was sitting at the bar and staring, lost in thought, at her gin and tonic. Cigarette smoke and the smell of spilled beer clung to the thick air. An old Metallica song was playing in the background and Lena sang along quietly.

A man in tight shorts and a checked shirt, who looked like a tourist, staggered over. 'A beautiful woman like you shouldn't be sitting here all alone,' he slurred, and an unpleasant waft of his boozy breath hit Lena in the face.

She forced a smile. 'Thanks, but I'm fine,' she said, hoping he would go away. But he was either too drunk to get the hint or he else he seemed not to want to get it, because he rested on the bar, close to Lena, and gave her a wry grin.

Lena rolled her eyes. *Oh, man, this is just what I fucking need after the day I've had* . . . She took her gin and tonic from the bar and turned her back on the man. He was determined not to be shaken off as easily as that and the next second Lena felt his hand on her shoulder.

'At least a drink, huh?' he whispered.

Lena recoiled. 'Get your fingers off me!'

But the drunk did not react. Lena would have been quite happy to knee him in the groin – she had handled much tougher types before – when a rotund guy of perhaps sixty left his place a couple of stools along at the bar and came over to join them. He pulled the drunk back by the arm.

'That's enough now—'

'Hey, man, what is this?' the drunk guy swore at him as he broke free. 'Keep out of it!'

Unexpectedly, the fat guy pulled a wallet out of his tattered jacket and held it open in front of his nose. 'See the ID here?'

'Aw, shit . . .' the man groaned dejectedly and admitted defeat.

'Exactly, so scram! And if I ever catch you here again bothering another lady, we'll continue our little conversation over at the station, get it?'

'All right . . .' The drunk lurched away.

'Thanks,' said Lena, smiling at the fat man.

'Yeah, yeah, no problem,' he muttered, stroked his stubbly chin and turned back to his double vodka on ice at the bar. 'One more,' he called to the bartender, who was covered in piercings, raising his glass.

'This one's on me,' said Lena.

'No, no, leave it – anyone would have done the same.'

She looked into his face, which was laced with scars. 'But no one else did.'

The fat man gave her a slight smile. 'You're probably the stubborn sort, eh?'

The bartender gave him another double vodka on ice and Lena another gin and tonic. 'It's on the house,' he mumbled, without looking her in the eye, and went back to washing glasses.

Smiling, Lena raised her glass to the man at her side.

'Well, what the hell,' he said, clinking glasses with hers.

'The trick with the police ID wasn't bad,' said Lena. 'How long were you with the police?'

He looked up from his drink. 'What do you mean *were*?'

'Your ID.' She grinned. 'It expired at the end of last year.'

His eyes widened in amazement. 'You're good. No one has noticed that before you.'

Lena took a long sip of her gin and tonic. 'I'm . . .' She corrected herself. 'I was also with the police . . . in some respects . . . until now at least.'

'Oh, really?' She seemed to have piqued his interest. 'You want to talk about it?'

Lena shook her head.

'And what next?' he asked.

She shrugged. 'No idea. I'm always just on the verge of doing my doctorate in Criminology, but then a case comes up and gets in the way, and I simply don't have the time.' She rubbed her forehead. 'I've had nothing but bad luck in this city – maybe I should make the most of the time off to go back home and have some peace and quiet to devote myself to my dissertation.'

The guy wheezed as he laughed. 'You can't have been all that lucky back there either, otherwise you would hardly have wound up in Berlin.'

'What do you mean?'

'All lost souls end up in Berlin sooner or later.'

'If you say so,' murmured Lena and raised her glass. 'To Berlin,' she said.

27

'*This* is where it's supposed to be?' Svenja Stollberg was visibly confused as she glanced around the foyer of the Beverly Inn.

In front of the reception desk stood a cheap standard lamp and a blue leatherette sofa on an orange felt carpet. She made no bones about having expected significantly more than this lower mid-range hotel, where everything was far less pretentious than the Hotel de Rome, or the Adlon or wherever it was that stars like Maloney normally stayed.

Artifex stopped and took the young reporter aside. 'Listen to me, love – maybe you're new to the business, but I've already told you: the swankier the hotel, the higher the risk that the paparazzi will be lurking,' he whispered to her, forcing himself not to stare constantly at her lips. 'Hollywood stars always reserve rooms at several hotels simultaneously, just in case one of the staff members takes a bribe. And besides, I never said that Maloney's staying here. Believe me, this is just for the party.' He laughed. 'This kind of place is ideal if all you're going to do is wreck the joint.' Artifex grinned at her. 'Rock 'n' roll, baby, you know?'

Stollberg did not seem convinced, but nodded anyway and followed him through the lobby. Artifex threw the two Eastern European-looking girls on the front desk a polite smile as they passed by. He took the room key out of the pocket of his jacket and headed straight for the lifts. Nobody in the hotel would get on to him, he thought, as they entered the lift. The reservation was not in his name and the police wouldn't find a body, not here anyway. The removal of the *labia oris* was an extremely complicated operation that required all his skills. It was certainly risky to carry out the procedure in a hotel room, but there was a certain kick that came with a change of scene. And after all, he had everything ready in advance to cover all eventualities; he had spread plenty of tarpaulin out across the room so as not to leave any bloodstains. He had heavy-duty duct tape to stifle her screams. Add to that the black bin bags and a suitcase just big enough to wheel Stollberg's corpse out of the room to his van. So far, everything had gone like clockwork, and he couldn't wait to finally be alone with the young woman. Still, he had to hurry, as Stollberg was already starting to get suspicious and seemed on the verge of losing her patience.

'You can bet your bottom dollar this is going to be an unforgettable party.' Artifex grinned when they stepped out of the lift a moment later on the third floor. He had to admit he was very amused by the fact that the pumped-up movie star was probably sitting in his jet on the way back to Los Angeles or wherever else, while this dumb little reporter would be sitting in the hotel room eagerly awaiting his arrival. It was a stroke of genius, he thought to himself, and he already had in mind the obituary that Stollberg's colleagues from *Star Biz* would publish on the occasion of her cruel demise.

28

When she entered room number 307, Svenja Stollberg was filled with a sudden sense of unease. 'Where are Maloney and the others?' Distraught, she peered around the empty room with its blue carpet, narrow wardrobe, minibar and double bed.

The man shrugged. 'Maybe they were stopped by a bunch of groupies,' he replied jokingly, shutting the door.

When Svenja Stollberg saw him turn the latch to lock it, she was filled with fear. She made a swift movement towards the door but her face turned as white as a sheet when she saw him with the syringe in his hand.

'Dear God! You're not a journalist!' Her voice trembled as the truth emerged with frightening clarity. She opened her mouth to scream but, before she knew it, the man had pressed her against the door with his elbow and clamped his hand across her mouth. She thrashed about and tried to bite his hand as he rammed the syringe into her shoulder through the gauzy fabric of her chiffon blouse. She managed to knee him in the balls and to rip the syringe out of her shoulder. She threw it as far as she could while the man doubled up, groaning in pain, and staggered back a couple of steps from the door.

Oh my God, get out of here quick! She fumbled to unlock the door and ran as fast as she could out of the room. But no sooner was she in the corridor than a numb sensation swept through her body. Whatever that bastard had injected her with seemed to take effect instantly. Her legs became heavier with each step. *Come on, keep going!* Her heart was racing as she dragged herself along the corridor. The lift, her salvation, was now just a few steps away. But despite fighting it with every fibre of her body, her legs would no longer obey her. She collapsed onto the carpet.

She summoned her last shred of strength to crawl that final stretch. The open lift door was barely an arm's length away. She was so close, almost there, when she suddenly felt him grab her by the legs. She wanted to scream, but only a croaking sound came out because her tongue was already paralysed. The next thing she knew, she was being dragged feet first back down the corridor and into the hotel room.

29

Thursday morning, 12th May

Since Lena had been withdrawn from the case, and she knew Volker Drescher often went to the gym, she preferred to go back to jogging outside. She certainly needed a bit of exercise today to clear her head and kill some time. As the sweat poured and her heart pounded, she forced herself to keep running. She passed the Märchenbrunnen fountain, the beach volleyball courts and the skateboard ramps in Friedrichshain Park. Lena crossed the road at the junction and jogged up the street until she stopped abruptly at a newspaper kiosk. Breathing deeply, she paused a moment to scan the headlines in the papers. After the news had spread like wildfire through the media the previous day – about the grisly death of a young journalist who had been found with a disfigured face in Tiergarten Park – it seemed that the gruesome serial killer had struck yet again.

MUTILATOR STRIKES AGAIN, read the headline of a major tabloid. Again, it was a woman from Berlin.

No, not again! Lena pulled some change out of her pocket and bought the newspaper.

'Your change!' the newspaper vendor shouted to her, but Lena was already briskly jogging home.

A short while later, she ran through the plain-looking inner courtyard of her apartment building, the newspaper and a bag of bread rolls tucked under her arm, when a blond, pale-looking man gave her a friendly wave. He was about Lena's age and was tinkering with his bike, which stood upside down, resting on the saddle.

'Hey, you must be the new neighbour!' He stood up and wiped his greasy hands on an old rag before he offered an out-stretched hand to Lena as she approached. He was wearing a T-shirt, army trousers cut off at the knees and some battered-looking Converse All Stars. 'Lukas Richter.'

Lena wiped her sweaty forehead with the sleeve of her hoody and returned his firm handshake. 'Lena Peters. I moved in a few days ago.'

'I know.' He grinned. 'I live just over there,' he said, nodding towards his apartment. 'If you need anything, just give me a shout. If I'm not in the rehearsal room, I'll just be sitting in front of the computer all day.'

Lena gave him a friendly smile. 'Will do.'

Nice guy, she thought as she ran on, fishing her apartment keys out of the pocket of her leggings.

30

No sooner had Lena closed her apartment door behind her than she spread the newspaper out next to the bag of bread rolls on the kitchen table and quickly scanned the article.

The body was found in the early hours of Thursday 12th May in the fen meadows by the River Tegel on the northern outskirts of Berlin. The body, which had decayed beyond recognition, was discovered at about twenty past midnight by a group of young walkers during a night hike through the nature reserve. First reports suggest the body had already been there for several weeks. Whether it is the thirty-year-old woman identified only as Suzanna W, who went missing about four weeks ago, is not yet clear.

Lena put some coffee on and wondered why there had been no mention this time of the manner in which this victim had been mutilated. Was it pure chance that this woman had been found so late, while previous victims had been found a few days or even hours after their deaths?

As the coffee was filtering through the percolator, Lena looked at the grainy photo printed next to the news item – a picture of Suzanna W taken few weeks before her disappearance. Why did the woman look so familiar? Deep in thought, Lena looked up.

The coffee was ready. She got a cup from the kitchen cupboard and poured herself some.

Whoever was behind these murders, Volker Drescher and his team would have to grapple with it by themselves now, she told herself as she sipped her coffee, still disappointed to have been withdrawn from the case. But she found she could not get the picture of this Suzanna W out of her head. She looked a lot like Suzanna – Suzanna Wirt. *Could it really be her?*

Lena dunked a bread roll into her black coffee, then went with the cup in hand into the living room, shaking her head. The chances that this dead woman could be Suzanna were almost vanishingly slim. And yet she could not shake off the thought. More for her own peace of mind than anything, Lena opened up her laptop on the dining table and started typing 'Suzanna W' into a search engine. *Suzanna Walde, chairman of the Dortmund Bowling Club . . . Suzanna Wartenberg, media consultant, Kaiserslautern . . . Facebook profile of Suzanna Weinert . . . Suzanna Winner Bach, Cologne Volunteers Fire Brigade . . .* Lena paused. *Suzanna Wirt, office administrator, Cenrat Media GmbH, Berlin*. It was the name of her best friend from school. Back then they had been inseparable, but after Suzanna had moved to Berlin with her parents, they lost contact. Lena put down her coffee cup. There were probably countless Suzanna Wirts in this city, she mused. She clicked through to the website of Cenrat Media all the same, in the hope of finding a photo of the employee. No such luck. Spurred on by this *idée fixe*, Lena spent hour after hour searching online for further clues. But her efforts were fruitless. By the time she closed the laptop again, it was already early afternoon.

Lena took a shower and stood a short while later in jeans and an olive green vest top in front of the refrigerator, which had only a half-eaten tin of ravioli to offer. With a sigh she let the refrigerator door swing shut and turned to her cat, who had slinked into the kitchen, meowing.

'Napoleon – I'd completely forgotten you, hadn't I?' She took a packet of cat food out of the cupboard, poured some into his bowl and put it down for him, along with a bowl of water. The tomcat immediately fell greedily upon his lunch. Smiling, Lena patted his dappled fur and her eyes lingered on him for a moment before she suddenly looked up. 'But of course!'

With a meow, Napoleon looked up from his bowl.

'I've got a photo of her,' said Lena, as though the animal could understand. She took a pair of scissors from the cutlery drawer, hurried back into the living room and quickly set about opening the cardboard box marked 'old photo albums and keepsakes'. This was the box where she had stowed away the very few items that offered a glimpse into her past. Lena was rifling through the various shoe boxes inside, when a photo, buried deep between yellowing love letters and tattered notebooks of poems from another life, fell into her hands: it was her twin sister Tamara. Although there had been many years of silence between them, Lena had recently left a message with her new Berlin address on Tamara's voicemail. As expected, Tamara had not returned her call. She was barely a couple of minutes younger than Lena, but after the death of their parents she had increasingly gone off the rails. Drugs and alcohol had dominated Tamara's life from early on, and it only got worse when she fell in with a dodgy crowd. Their overstretched foster parents had placed her in a boarding school for maladjusted teenagers, which proved to be a terrible mistake, because it was there that things went from bad to worse. Later, she was always getting involved with the wrong man. Again, the images of that awful scene in Tamara's apartment shot through Lena's mind. Lena had only wanted to help and had no idea back then that that day would cast a shadow over the rest of their lives. She shook her head, trying not to think about it. Although she had now resigned herself to the fact that it was for the best that they had no more contact, seeing a picture of her twin sister still felt like a stab in the heart. She forced herself to push the thought aside and went back to rummaging through the box. Certificates. Photos of her on her first day of school, holding her *Schultüte* cone outside the school building. Photos of her on a school trip. Memories filled her mind. Lena put the photos aside and rummaged deeper, until she finally found the photo album she had been looking for. She quickly flipped through the pages. When she came to a photo taken at a swimming championship, she stopped. Lena stood amid a group of teenagers grinning into the camera. She ran her forefinger along the names written out below it: Corinna Radusch, Alexander Köstner, Melanie Stockheim, Annemarie Grosse, Viktor Rudolf. Her finger stopped. Suzanna Wirt. Lena studied the picture closely. With the album in her hand, she went back to the kitchen and compared the photo with the image of the now-dead woman in the newspaper spread out on the table. She could not deny the resemblance. But the quality of both images was too bad to confirm a definite match. Lena knew she would not get any peace until she knew for sure. And she already had an idea of how she would be able to find out the identity of the dead woman. If there was a chance it was actually her old friend, she would stay in Berlin for as long as it took until the case was solved. She owed Suzanna Wirt that much. She quickly put the contents of the memories box away again, grabbed her trench coat from the wardrobe and hurried out the front door.

31

At around 5.30 p.m., Lena parked her scooter in front of the
Institute of Forensic Medicine in Moabit. She stowed her helmet away and walked quickly through the grounds of the former municipal hospital, flashed her ID card at the porter and
disappeared in through the entrance to Forensic Pathology.
Lena strode purposefully towards the autopsy room. The clas-
sical music she could hear from the corridor told her that
Dr Kurt Böttner was the pathologist on-duty. Böttner never
worked without music; the silence of the dead would drive
him out of his mind, as he had told Lena on her previous visit
to Pathology.

'Hello, Dr Böttner,' said Lena, stepping into the sterile,
harshly illuminated room, as the electric sliding door whirred
shut behind her.

The coroner, a man of about fifty with thinning reddish hair
tied into a wispy ponytail at the nape of his neck, stood in his
lab coat at the examination table, bent over a highly decom-
posed body whose chest cavity he had already opened. He
looked up briefly and nodded to her, before continuing with
the autopsy. Lena stayed a good half metre from the dissection
table. Although it was quite routine for her to go into Pathology,
the sight of mortal remains still made her stomach churn. The

extracted organs such as the liver and heart, which lay in individual metal bowls, were as hard to stomach as the putrid smell that filled the room.

'Is this her?' Lena asked with self-assuredness intended to suggest that she was still on Drescher's team.

'As far as I know, you've been taken off the case,' replied Dr Böttner. 'You shouldn't be here.'

Damn, she should have known that the news would have already gone around that she'd been suspended! What had she expected?

She buried her hands in her pockets and looked at Böttner with a guilty expression. 'I know,' she admitted, and gave him a wry smile. 'But if the dead woman is indeed the missing Suzanna W, I might be able to identify her.'

'Tell Drescher that, not me. I'm just doing my job here.' He let out a sudden chuckle. 'Besides, you'd have to be a clairvoyant to be able to identify someone in this state. Apart from a few shreds of rotten tissue, the muddy hair stuck to the skull is about the only thing the rodents and maggots have left behind.'

Lena nodded and felt the nausea rise in her again. In fact, it was hard to guess from the corpse whether it was female or male, let alone whether it was her friend Suzanna.

'In the papers the victim is ascribed to the Mutilator – what kind of mutilation are we talking about?'

Böttner sighed. 'You never give up, huh?'

Instead of giving an answer, Lena just grinned.

'OK,' he groaned, casually placing his scalpel in a tray on the surgical instruments trolley, and finally offering her a bowl of menthol paste.

Lena had to lean in closer to the body. The paste, which they smeared under their noses, could mask the smell, but did nothing for the feeling of disgust and revulsion that the sight prompted.

'Just so we understand each other properly – anything you learn from me is no more than you would read in the papers in the next few days anyway,' Böttner clarified, and with a jerk of his hand he pulled away the bright green cloth that was covering the body from the abdomen down. 'Does this answer your question?'

Lena had to swallow and felt her stomach roil violently. *Come on, pull yourself together!* For a moment she desperately tried to block out the whole autopsy room around her, with all its lights and smells, and to focus on the body. *Why just her feet?* she wondered.

'Why are her feet any different to those of Yvonne Novak . . . ?' she murmured absently to herself.

The coroner looked at her askance. 'What do you mean?'

Lena answered his question with a question. 'What shoe size would this person have been?'

He put on a thoughtful expression. 'Good question. Her height is one metre sixty-seven . . .' He glanced over at the X-rays he had made of the skeleton and then looked back at the corpse on the examination table.

'Maybe thirty-seven or thirty-eight. Can't say for certain.'

Lena nodded. 'It turned out that the previous victim, Yvonne Novak, was size thirty-nine, which apparently wasn't what the perpetrator was after, otherwise he would hardly have chucked her feet casually into the Spree.'

Böttner frowned. 'That's why with Novak he just kept the legs.'

Lena thought. 'He's very picky and he clearly observes his victims closely in advance.'

'You mean the victims knew their killer?'

'It's very possible,' Lena mused, and looked back down at the rotting corpse on the autopsy table.

'Have you been able to determine what the cause of death was?' asked Lena.

Böttner scratched his clean-shaven chin. 'The victim is most likely to have bled to death from the amputation, like the others. We need to see the toxicological and the forensic chemistry results first before we can be sure.' He walked round to the foot of the table and gestured to Lena.

'Look at that. Isn't it amazing – the precision with which he has severed the feet?' His tone was almost reverent, while Lena could feel every fibre of her body positively resisting, holding her back from looking.

'He must have used a bone saw,' explained Dr Böttner, opening a drawer on the trolley. 'Something like this here.' He held up a saw, which was a good forty centimetres long, then put it back in the drawer.

'And who would own a saw like that?'

'Theoretically, anyone could.' He pulled the cloth back over the legs of the corpse and laughed. 'It's not just in surgery that bone saws are used – you'd find one in any good restaurant or a butcher's shop.'

Lena nodded and let his words sink in while Böttner went back to removing the lungs, right before her eyes.

'May I use your toilet?' asked Lena, clearing her throat with a cough.

'Along the corridor, first door on the right,' said Böttner, unable to resist a mischievous grin. 'Feeling sick?'

'No,' Lena said firmly and disappeared in the direction of the toilet.

She had barely closed the door before the burger, which she had quickly scoffed down on the way, lay at the bottom of the toilet bowl. Lena pressed the flush and went over to the sink. She rinsed out her mouth and wiped it with a rough paper towel. Then she saw it again: blood! Blood everywhere, all over her hands! Lena's heart was pounding. *The soap dispenser, quick!* Manically she washed her hands, over and over, with great quantities of soap. She scrubbed her fingers roughly under the tap until her skin burned and she finally managed to dispel the awful memories. Breathless, she slumped against the cool tile wall and crouched down on the floor.

Breathe deeply. In and out . . . in and out . . . Finally she got up and straightened her back before she stepped outside again.

'Tell me, could the victim not be identified by a tooth comparison?' she enquired when she returned to the autopsy room.

'Not yet,' said Dr Böttner, who was putting on a new CD.

Lena did not believe him.

'Frau Peters, I think it's time for you to leave,' he added impatiently.

Lena peered at him suspiciously. 'OK.' She was just about to disappear through the door when she paused not far from the door labelled 'CT – Magnetic Resonance Imaging'. She span around on her heel. 'But I presume you've done a facial reconstruction?'

The coroner gave her an annoyed glare. As soon as he saw that Lena was heading towards the door in question, Dr Böttner hurried over with his long stride and turned her away with outstretched arms.

'You have no authority to enter!'

'Listen, I need to know if this dead body is my friend!'

'Either you leave now or I will be forced to call Security!'

Lena slumped her shoulders. 'OK, you win . . . I'm going.' She walked towards the exit, only to turn the second the coroner stepped away from the door, and dash as fast as she could into the room.

'GODDAMMIT, PETERS!' She heard Dr Böttner roar. But before he could catch her, Lena glimpsed the images of the head, reconstructed with the help of 3D visualisation, on the large computer monitor straight ahead. The facial features had been generated with high-resolution spatial image files and showed every tiny detail.

Lena gasped. *Oh God!* She stared at the face of Suzanna.

'Out!' shouted Böttner, dragging Lena by the arm. 'The security guards will be here any minute!'

Lena pulled herself free.

32

Spring in Berlin had been much cooler this year than expected, and the long-awaited increase in temperature was still yet to materialise. Lena turned up her collar as the rain started to fall while she stood outside the grey building of the institute. Angry with Böttner, she was determined not to give up so easily. Next, she wanted to take Ferdinand Roggendorf to task again. Lena did not believe Roggendorf was the culprit. The infamous Mutilator went about his business in a very controlled way with the utmost precision; he was certainly not an impulsive, easily provoked hothead like Roggendorf. Nevertheless, Lena needed to be certain.

A glance at her watch reminded her that Roggendorf went to his boxing club every Thursday night at about this time. There was surely nothing wrong with checking that out.

Deciding to leave her scooter behind because of the rain, Lena hailed a taxi.

'I need to go to a boxing club called The Steel Fist – have you heard of it?' she asked the driver, getting into the back seat.

The Mediterranean-looking man, whose shirt was unbuttoned to reveal his bushy chest hair, turned to face her with a grin on his lips.

'Of course I know it,' he said with a Turkish accent. He turned on the meter and steered back onto the road. 'You sure you want go there?' He peered at Lena in the rear-view mirror, as if wondering why on earth she would want to go to such a dive.

'Quite sure.'

The driver turned off at the next junction towards Spandau. After a while they had left the city centre far behind and, block by block, the buildings started to look more and more dilapidated. As the sum on the meter rose higher and higher, it started to feel to Lena as if she had already spent an eternity in this taxi. After a good forty minutes, the driver pulled up on the right.

'That's twenty-seven euros. Do you want a receipt?'

'Thank you, no need.' She handed him three ten euro bills. 'Keep the change.'

When she got out of the taxi, it had stopped raining. Lena looked at her watch again. Roggendorf wouldn't be here until 7 o'clock. On the spur of the moment, she decided to pop into the small Thai diner across the road to stop her stomach from rumbling. It stank of stale fat and one glimpse into the open kitchen revealed that this business was undoubtedly a case for the health and safety inspector. The Asian chef, who had a burned-down cigarette in his mouth as he chucked a handful of beansprouts into a pan, seemed as indifferent to this as the puffy-faced men drinking beer at the next table who turned to stare at Lena. Since she had not seen anywhere else to get a bite to eat in the area, and her empty stomach was again drawing attention to itself, she decided to stay. Besides, she could keep an eye on the entrance to the boxing club from here.

Lena sat down on the bench with its sticky plastic cushion and ordered a chicken curry, which, as it turned out, was not so bad after all. While she ate, she glanced up every now and then at the boxing club over the road.

It was getting dark when, some time later, Ferdinand Roggendorf appeared. When Lena saw him disappear inside, she threw her napkin onto her plate and paid. She had just stepped out of the diner when she spotted Roggendorf coming back out of the club with a sports bag in his hand.

That was a quick visit, Lena thought. *You definitely didn't do any boxing.* She crossed the road and followed him, keeping a certain distance, past dark doorways where dealers were standing around in small groups, going about their business. Young men sat on kerbs, drinking beer. Lena could sense the stares. She speeded up and followed Roggendorf into a gloomy side street at the end of which was an abandoned-looking industrial site. 'Spandau Staaken Former Gasworks' she read on the sign in front of the dilapidated entrance.

What on earth is he up to? But before she knew it, she had lost sight of Roggendorf. Lena looked around, a sick feeling in her stomach. Before her lay the disused factory – an eerie setting in the fading sunlight. The walls were sprayed with graffiti, the windows smashed. *Whatever Roggendorf's doing here, it's definitely something dodgy.*

Ignoring the 'No Trespassing! Danger!' sign, she carefully stepped over the trampled-down barbed wire fence, then she noticed the flicker of a torch. Something made Lena hesitate before she entered the overgrown site, which nature had reconquered over the years. Inside the ruined building, it looked just as desolate. The roof had largely collapsed. The floor was in pieces. Here and there, a whiff of ammonia and sulphur ran through the cool air. Lena had difficulty avoiding the gas cylinders that were lying around, labelled with faded pictograms, including skull and crossbones. Lena kept looking around, paying attention to every sound and shadow. Then she saw the beam of the torch again – by the bottling equipment at the other end of the hall. She walked up a rickety iron staircase to a platform leading to a series of huge tanks. She held her breath as she walked around them. But she didn't see any movement behind them. She was feeling uneasy and wondering whether coming here had been a good idea, when suddenly she stubbed her toe on a steel chain lying on the floor, which rattled so loudly that it would certainly be heard throughout the hall.

'*Shit!*' Lena whispered, and the next moment she heard a loud clanking sound – coming from the back door. Lena dashed that way. She reached the back door, which stood ajar, and led to the abandoned factory yard. She pressed herself against the crumbling wall of the factory building and listened carefully. Nothing but the quiet of the evening. Her gaze wandered over the metre-high chimneys that rose up between the bushes, lined up in a row like silent toy soldiers. There was no sign of Roggendorf. Lena looked around and hurried along the side of the unlit factory building and across the courtyard, when suddenly by the corner of the entrance hall she heard the roar of a car engine. She heard wheels spinning on the sandy earth and before she could jump aside, the car hit her. The force of the impact hurled her onto the ground as the car screeched to a standstill. Lena lay there, paralysed. Everything was spinning. The smell of burned rubber filled her nose. Suddenly the torch flashed on and her heart pounded against her ribs when she heard the car door open and the driver approach. The glare of the torchlight was directed straight at her face.

'*You?* Jesus! Are you hurt?'

Lena took a while to realise that the voice belonged to the former policeman with the scarred face, whose acquaintance she had made the other evening in the pub.

'I . . . I'm . . . not sure,' Lena croaked, shielding her eyes with her hand against the dazzling light. It took a moment until her field of vision cleared again.

'Can you stand up?' he asked with a cigarette in his mouth.

'I'll try,' she moaned and slowly got up. Fortunately, nothing seemed to be broken. She was shaken, but it was a lucky escape.

'Can I not leave you out of my sight for a second before you get into some kind of trouble?!' the guy growled as he helped her up.

'Hey, give me a break! You just ran me over! What are you doing here anyway? And why in God's name are you driving without any lights on?'

He laughed huskily. 'If I had wanted Roggendorf to see me, I'd have put the old blue light on the roof.'

Lena remained suspicious. 'How do you know Ferdinand Roggendorf?'

He buried his hands in his pockets and put his cigarette out with his foot. 'None of your business.'

Lena gasped. 'I think I probably have a right to know what you're up to!'

Clearing his throat, the man looked around him. 'This isn't exactly the best area to hang around in as a woman, which rather raises the question of what *you're* up to.' He scratched his head. 'Come on, get in, I'll give you a lift.'

Lena hesitated.

'What? Do I look like a serial killer?' he asked jokingly, as he noticed her hesitation.

Well. She scrutinised him for a moment.

'Wouldn't I have just run you over after all, if I was?' He gestured encouragingly to her. 'Come on, I haven't got the time or the slightest desire to stand around here any longer!'

OK then. Lena got into the green Peugeot.

33

'Come on then, out with it – what were you up to?' the man repeated his question as he steered out of the factory yard.

'Investigations,' Lena replied tersely and returned the question: 'And you?'

He drove towards the lit alleyway where Lena had followed Roggendorf. 'The same, I guess.'

Lena remained sceptical. 'I thought you were long retired?'

He turned to her and gave her a smile. 'And didn't you say you'd been taken off the case?'

'It's something personal . . .' She leaned back in the seat with her arms folded and inhaled the cool breeze that streamed in through the open window. 'And you?'

'Ditto,' murmured the man. He steered the car onto the main road, reached for a box of cigarettes and held it out to Lena. 'Do you smoke?'

She shook her head. 'No, thanks. I stopped two months ago.'

He grinned and lit up. 'I started again two months ago – after sixteen years.'

Lena looked at him, but said nothing.

'I'm Wulf Belling, by the way.'

'Lena Peters,' she said, nodding to him with a smile. But Belling looked straight ahead again, as if he were suddenly afraid of the ice melting.

'You can drop me at the next S-Bahn station,' Lena said after a while, and went back to looking out of the window.

'Are you sure? Where do you need to get to?'

'Moabit – the Institute of Forensic Medicine. I left my scooter there.'

'You're sure you don't want me to drop you off there?'

'I'll be fine.'

'Don't tell me you've got another appointment?'

She shook her head. 'No . . . that's for sure . . .'

They drove straight on. Lena glanced at the barren high-rise blocks, which all looked so alike.

'My wife left me a few months ago and my daughter is still holding it against me – so there's nothing waiting for me besides a good old-fashioned nightcap.' His cigarette bobbed up and down as he spoke, and there was sadness in his eyes.

'And were you to blame?'

He looked at her, a little confused.

'I mean, for the separation. Were you in the wrong or not?'

He drummed his chunky fingers on the steering wheel. 'Well, it depends on how you look at it . . . I'd say maybe I wasn't entirely blame-free. It was this accursed case – I just couldn't get it out of my head . . .'

Silently, Lena nodded. She knew only too well what he was talking about.

'It's possible that I neglected Helena once or twice, but somehow I presumed she'd be OK with it – it was for a good cause, after all.' He flicked the ash from his cigarette out of the window. 'For months on end I tried to put a stop to this bastard, but every time I was nearly there he'd vanish into thin air again – as though someone had warned him at the last minute. And within no time at all, there'd be a new mutilated corpse.' He threw his cigarette butt out the window.

Lena turned to face him.

'Then the case was passed onto this real flash Harry from Homicide and I was sent into early retirement because of my "ruthless approach" or some other totally absurd pretext,' Belling continued. He tapped his finger against his forehead. 'You know what my theory is? Someone just wanted me out of the way . . .'

Precisely like Dr Cornelia Dobelli, it occurred to Lena.

'It looks like you can't put the case behind you,' she remarked. 'Otherwise you would hardly be shadowing Ferdinand Roggendorf.'

Suddenly he slammed on the brakes and stopped in the middle of the road.

Startled, Lena clung to her seatbelt.

'I'm a father. I have a daughter,' he said, clearly enraged. 'And just the thought that she might run into him sends a cold shiver down my spine.' His gaze was fierce.

Lena nodded, looking tensely into the rear-view mirror, waiting for Belling to drive off before he caused a rear-end collision.

'So I've set myself the task of catching this bastard before I kick the bucket,' he said. 'Fuck it – I don't care if it's the last thing I do in this shitty life.' Finally he drove off again.

'And what makes you so sure it's Roggendorf?'

'Let's just say I have my sources. And it can't be denied that he's not quite kosher . . .'

'Still, that proves nothing at all,' said Lena.

The stocky man frowned angrily. 'Perhaps I'm not hearing right – what kind of a contract have you got with the precious lawyer's boy?'

Lena took a deep breath. 'None. But he just doesn't fit the profile. I only want to make sure the right person is put behind bars.'

'I see . . .' Shortly after, he stopped at S-Bahn station. 'Will you be OK?'

Lena nodded and got out. 'Thanks,' she added and slammed the car door.

'Oh . . . um . . .'

She leaned down to the open window. 'Yes?'

'Here . . .' He handed her a business card.

Detective Chief Superintendent Wulf Belling, Ninth Station.

'It's not quite up to date – but the mobile number is still right, and . . . um . . . if you get the bright idea of prowling around some dodgy area at night or fancy getting run over by someone, then just give me a call.'

Lena couldn't help but smile. 'Will do.'

She put his card in her pocket and walked down the steps to the S-Bahn.

34

Lena was sitting at home in front of her laptop. The fact that Drescher was keeping Dr Dobelli's investigation file under lock and key would not stop bothering her and suggested to her that he knew far more about the case than he was willing to admit. So she spent the whole afternoon scouring the internet for information about Volker Drescher – anything that could hint at his involvement in the case. However, as she had suspected, she found nothing but a flawless record. Drescher had an impeccable CV and had served more than twenty successful years in the police force. His books were all bestsellers. Moreover, he regularly donated considerable sums to the SOS Children's Villages and was an active member of the charity Victims Against Violence. All other avenues of research kept coming to a dead end.

Lena went to the homicide division website and logged into her mailbox. Intrigued, she clicked on the group email with the subject '*New evidence re suspect Roggendorf hair*', which had been circulated to members of the department. But the email would not open. '*ACCESS DENIED*'. She tried again, and again the warning popped up.

'Shit!' The doorbell rang. Lena looked up in surprise. She was not expecting anyone. After another buzz, Napoleon jumped down from the sofa and sprinted out of the room. Lena stood up, walked down the hall and opened the door. There stood her neighbour, Lukas Richter, grinning and holding up a six-pack of beer.

'I saw you were home – and I remembered, we haven't had a drink yet to toast being neighbours!'

Lena smiled. She was too busy really, but on the other hand she had reached an impasse for the moment anyway. A cold beer was right on cue. Besides, there was something about Lukas that she quite liked.

'Then it's probably high time.' She took the six-pack from him, stepped back and held the door open for him with another smile. They went into the kitchen and Lena opened two bottles of beer. She put the rest in the fridge.

'What?' she asked with an uncertain smile when she saw his shocked expression as he glanced at the fridge.

'Good god, what . . . what's all this? Other people put up pictures of living people in their flats – but you're more into dead people by the looks of it?'

'Oh, that . . . It's an occupational hazard, I guess,' said Lena, embarrassed as she followed his gaze to the photos of the dead women. To change the subject, she proposed a toast. 'Well, here's to being neighbours – cheers!'

Still a little vexed, he looked at Lena. Then his face brightened. 'Let's have a toast as friends, not just neighbours,' he proposed with a smile as he raised his bottle. 'Somehow I had a feeling you were with the police!'

'In a way,' she replied and took a sip of beer.

'Let me guess, you're a secret agent or something like that?'

She laughed. 'Not quite.'

'What then?'

Lena looked at him. She barely knew Lukas and she was normally very reticent when a stranger was inquisitive in this way, but with him there was something different. She somehow had the feeling that she'd known him for ever. She took Lukas into the living room while she gave him a rough summary of what had happened to her in the last few days, without going into too much detail.

'Sounds as if the whole thing's a bit crazy,' said Lukas, as his eyes wandered inquisitively around the room.

'You could say that . . .' Lena answered, sitting back on the sofa with a sigh.

'Here, perhaps this will cheer you up a bit,' he said, pulling a flyer out from the side pocket of his army trousers and handing it to her.

'The Preachers,' Lena read, sensing Lukas' expectant gaze on her.

'We've got a gig tonight at the Kings Club. I'm on the drums. Come along.'

'Thanks, I'll see . . .' she said evasively and put the flyer on the glass coffee table. Lukas nodded. *He almost looks a bit disappointed*, Lena thought.

'I'll put you on the guest list anyway,' he suggested. 'Then you can decide later.'

Lena gave him a fleeting smile.

Then he asked, 'Can I use your toilet?'

'Sure.'

Lukas stood up and Lena watched him as he left the room.

'Oh man, you've even got those gross photos in your bathroom!' he said in horror when he came back. 'Can you really sleep at night surrounded by all these dead bodies?' he asked, as he carried on looking around the living room.

'I don't see dead bodies, I just see the message the perpetrator was trying to convey with his actions.'

'Hmm. Well, anyway . . . I mean, oh man, everywhere you look in this place, you just see crime and death and blood.'

She looked at him and thought about his words. He was right. If she wasn't careful, she would slowly but surely turn into a fanatic like Wulf Belling.

'Is that your daughter?' he asked after casually pulling a framed photograph out of one of the boxes she had left open while unpacking.

'No, no,' Lena said, smiling. She stood up and walked over to him with the beer bottle in her hand. 'Fabienne is my adorable little niece,' she said, taking the photo out of his hand.

'She looks a hell of a lot like you.'

'That's probably because my sister and I are identical twins,' she replied with a forced smile.

'You have a twin sister? That's awesome . . . Does she live in Berlin too?'

Lena shook her head. 'We're not really in touch.' She quickly put the picture back in the box.

'Really? Why's that?'

'Believe me, it's better that way.' But deep inside, Lena still felt a kind of pain at losing Tamara, even though she would never admit it.

Instead of sitting down again, Lukas glanced at the screen of her laptop, which was still open on the dining table. Lena followed him. 'Look, I've still got a lot to do and . . .'

'Wow, what have we got here?' Lukas gleefully clapped his hands together. 'Looks like you've had access to your account blocked.'

Lena raised her eyebrows and slammed the laptop shut. 'I don't think that's any of your business.'

Lukas stared at her. Suddenly a cheeky grin flitted across his face. 'I could reactivate access to your account, at least temporarily . . .' He rubbed his hands together excitedly. 'May I?' Without waiting to see Lena's reaction, he had opened the laptop up again and his fingers were darting about over the keyboard at the speed of light.

'Hey, what are you doing?'

'It's just a little workaround to get the administrative privileges,' he said nonchalantly, tapping away at the keys. A few moments later, he snapped his fingers. '*Et voilà!* I guess this is the email you wanted to read?'

Astonished, Lena stared over his shoulder. 'Not bad. How did you do that?'

'I know what I'm doing with computers – and that was pretty straightforward.' He stepped aside and left the laptop to Lena. 'Well then, I'd probably better excuse myself – and if you ever need any help, you know where to find me.'

Her face brightened up. 'Yeah, er . . . thank you,' she said, still rather flummoxed, and gave him a grateful smile.

'Don't worry, I'll let myself out.'

Lena's eyes were already scanning the email, transfixed, when Lukas stopped at the front door and turned. Lena looked up, her brow furrowed. There was something unsettling about the way he looked at her with his piercing blue eyes.

'Next time, it'll cost you more than a pretty smile . . .' he said with a mischievous grin.

Before Lena could reply, Lukas had already closed the door behind him.

He's a cheeky one, that Lukas, she thought, before she impatiently turned her attention back to the email on her screen.

'*On his father's advice, Ferdinand Roggendorf has since admitted having hosted satanic gatherings at his dacha, which Yvonne Novak occasionally attended.* Lena raised her eyebrows. So that much was true. *Nevertheless, he still claims to have nothing to do with the murders,* she read on, rubbing her temples reflectively.

What if Suzanna Wirt had also been to Roggendorf's dacha at some point before her death? To find this out, she had just one choice: she needed to find out who Suzanna had been associated with most recently, who her friends were and her enemies. Perhaps there was some kind of connection to Ferdinand Roggendorf after all. Lena brought up the Cenrat Media website again. Maybe she could find out more from Suzanna's boss. And she also wanted to take Belling with her to try and see Suzanna's parents.

35

Early evening, north of Berlin

A flock of birds flew overhead squawking. Then all was silent again. Almost silent, anyway – the only sounds were the rustle of leaves and the fluttering of the crime scene tape. Lena was lying on the ground at the edge of the fen. She lay completely rigid on her back, like a corpse. Her eyes were closed, she felt the damp earth under her palms. She smelled the slightly putrid odour rising from the boggy ground.

Were you already dead when he left you here last month? Or was your heart still beating?

A slight breeze blew a strand of hair onto her face and she felt a few blades of grass tickling her ears as the phone in her pocket started ringing. Lena opened her eyes. She pushed herself up with one hand and took the call.

'Yes, Peters speaking.' Just a few metres away she spotted Wulf Belling. He stood with his back to her on the other side of the police cordon, halfway to the car park.

'Frau Peters, where are you?' she heard him say. 'If we're going to visit your school friend's mother then we're going to need to get a move on.'

'I'm over here,' she called to him.

Aghast, Belling glanced over at her, a cigarette dangling from his mouth. 'Jesus Christ, what are you doing?'

Lena stood up and brushed the dirt from her trench coat. 'According to the police cordon, Suzanna Wirt must have been found about here.' She ducked back under the red and white barrier tape and walked towards Belling. 'And right there, there's supposed to be a building site,' she said, pointing a finger at the makeshift fence that bordered the fen.

Belling stamped out his cigarette and took the leaflet Lena handed him. 'It says here the fens were supposed to be drained about a month ago.'

'Which was cancelled at the last minute after massive protests by conservationists,' Lena added.

Belling dropped the hand holding the leaflet. 'And which the perpetrator could hardly have foreseen when he left Suzanna Wirt's body here,' he continued, gazing at the fens around him. 'Suggesting that, even this time, he intended for the dead woman to be found.'

She put her hands on her hips. 'Looks like it.'

'How far is it from here to the Wirts' place?'

'Just under two kilometres.' Lena pointed to the footpath that trailed through the nature reserve. 'I've walked along it. At normal walking pace it takes about twenty minutes. Suzanna's mother told me on the phone that her daughter used to come here jogging a lot – in which case you could do it in ten minutes easily.'

He nodded. 'And if you were running away from someone in fear for your life, you'd probably be even faster.'

Lena looked back at the path and considered Belling's words.

'How did you get hold of the Wirts' address, anyway?' he asked, as Lena followed him to the car park where he had left his green Peugeot. Lena had left her Vespa a bit further away.

'I called Cenrat Media and asked. When I told them I was an old friend of Suzanna's, the head of HR gave me her mum's phone number. So I gave her a call and she still remembered me from before . . .'

'I see,' he muttered and pointed over at his car with his thumb. 'Come on, get in, we can pass by here again later for you to pick up your scooter.'

'OK,' said Lena, walking towards the car. 'Just follow the road along and the Wirts' house will be on the right,' she said when she was sitting in the passenger seat.

Belling did as instructed and drove along the bumpy dirt track back up to the main road, while Lena looked out for the house that lay in this desolate area at the edge of a small suburb. The closer they got to the Wirts' house, the more uncomfortable she felt about meeting Ariane Wirt. Not only because of Suzanna's death, but also because this visit meant confronting her own past. It was two decades since she last saw Ariane Wirt back in Fischbach. At that time, everything was still fine in Lena's world. She had enjoyed a comfortable childhood in a loving family home. She had lots of friends. She was a straight-A student. But after the death of her parents and the separation from her twin sister, her life lost its equilibrium. Lena cut herself off more and more from everything around her. She shunned her peers for fear they might start talking to her about her dead parents. Her academic performance went downhill rapidly, and it was only when she was a bit older that Lena started to get her ambition and sense of purpose back.

A strange noise suddenly tore Lena from her thoughts and catapulted her abruptly back into the present.

'What was that?' The next moment, she heard a rustling announcement that sounded like a radio message. To her surprise, she discovered a walkie-talkie on the shelf beneath the dashboard. 'You're listening into police radio?'

Wulf Belling pursed his lips. 'Oh, just now and again . . .'

'That's illegal, you know,' said Lena, and suppressed a grin.

This man is nothing but surprises, she thought and turned to look out of the window again.

36

'The address is right,' Lena said as they stood on the Wirts' doorstep a short while later. The simple, once whitewashed family house looked in need of renovation. Except for the enthusiastically waving garden gnomes standing on the gravel in front of the house, there was nothing particularly welcoming about the house.

'How . . . how do I look?' asked Belling suddenly.

Lena turned to face him as her index finger reached for the bell. Only now did she notice that he had had his hair cut. He had swapped his worn-out loafers for a pair of leather shoes, and his trousers matched his new-looking corduroy jacket. Even his shirt was carefully ironed.

'Is it that important?' she asked him, somewhat perplexed.

He hemmed and hawed. 'Well . . . I'm meeting Helena afterwards.'

'Ah, your ex-wife?' Lena asked with a puzzled smile. 'How come?'

'I honestly have no idea.' He buried his hands in his beige corduroy trousers and shrugged his shoulders. 'Maybe she just had a weak moment or something . . . Anyway, she called me and said it was about time to talk. Sounds sensible, right?'

Lena saw that he looked at the wedding ring on his finger. He still always wore it. His ex-wife obviously meant more to him than he cared to admit.

'We're meeting in our old local,' he told her, his cheeks burning. He smiled, lost in thought. 'You won't believe it, but it's more than forty years since we met there for the first time – and it's still the same pub. I bet they haven't even changed the tablecloths.'

Lena had to smile. When she rang the bell again, the front door opened this time.

Ariane Wirt stood at the doorway in her slippers with a tea towel in her hand. Her eyes were red and swollen. She had clearly been crying. She wore a dark sweater, which looked hand-knitted, and a well-worn pleated skirt.

'Hello, Frau Wirt. I'm sorry that we meet again in such circumstances.' Lena reached her hand out to Ariane Wirt with a sense of being an old friend.

'It's good to see you again after so long,' said Ariane Wirt, as she wiped her wet hands on the tea towel and shook hands with Lena. Her handshake was limp, like that of an old lady. And straight away Lena sensed the despair that lay behind the brave smile Suzanna's mother was putting on.

'When I last saw you, you and Suzanna were still at school.'

Lena smiled at her. 'Yes, it really was a long time ago . . .' She pointed to Belling. 'This is Wulf Belling . . . my . . . my partner,' she said quickly.

Belling nodded eagerly, and Ariane Wirt invited them in. After a glance at the street to check they had not been followed, Frau Wirt closed the door. 'I've taken our name off the bell

to stop the press asking questions, about Suzanna I mean . . .'
Frau Wirt shuffled ahead in her slippers as Lena and Belling
followed her along the hallway, where the walls were decked in
dusty medals and childhood photos. The house had the musty
smell of old carpets. From the inside it seemed much smaller
than it did from the outside, which Lena attributed to the huge
antique furniture crammed into the rooms. It felt a lot like a
junk shop.

'That's sensible,' said Lena as they arrived in the kitchen. This
room was also full of dark furniture from a bygone age. Large
windows looked over the overgrown back garden.

'Tea?'

'Please,' said Lena, taking a seat at the kitchen table alongside
Belling.

'Still with lots of sugar and a dash of milk?'

Lena smiled. 'Milk yes, sugar no.'

'And for you, Herr Belling?'

It was a second or two before Belling looked up and registered that she was speaking to him, as if in his mind he was
already on his date with his ex-wife. 'Uh, thank you, nothing
for me.'

Suzanna's mother put some water out. 'So you're with the
police.'

'In a way, yes . . .' Lena replied.

'Yesterday someone else came from the police.' She took a cup
and a box of tea bags out of the kitchen cupboard. 'A man, not
very tall. What was his name now . . . ?'

Not very tall? thought Lena, her ears pricking up. 'Drescher,
perhaps?' she asked in surprise.

'Yes, that's right.'

Lena exchanged a confused look with Belling. Why did the head of Homicide pay Ariane a visit personally when he had a team of staff to do that for him?

As Lena thought about it, Ariane Wirt took down a framed picture from the windowsill, of Suzanna at the 1989 swimming championships. 'Do you remember, you used to often swim together at the outdoor pool in the summer?' With tears in her eyes, she handed Lena the photograph.

Lena looked down at the photo. 'And sometimes we used to go to the lake on the weekend.'

'How old would you have been then? Twelve? Thirteen?' mused Frau Wirt with a sad smile.

'Could be,' said Lena, seeing her try to be strong and to fight back the tears. To see Ariane Wirt suffer like this was awful. If a mother has her child taken from her, especially her only child, Lena knew the emotional pain was indescribable. Besides, with such an unimaginably cruel, violent crime, as in the case of Suzanna Wirt, it was often tremendously difficult for the survivors to accept what had happened. Added to this was the uncertainty about the circumstances of the crime, which significantly complicated the process of grieving. How did she die exactly? How long did she suffer? Lena knew these questions often plagued the bereaved to the end of their life and often led to post-traumatic stress disorder.

She passed the picture on to Belling, as Ariane Wirt nodded her head at the chair Lena was sitting on.

'I still can't believe that my Suzanna is dead. I mean, just a couple of weeks ago she was sitting here at the table.' She poured some pills into her hand from a small pot that was on the shelf and washed them down with a glass of water. 'Without these things I would have probably gone out of my mind – slowly but surely,' she admitted with a forced laugh when she noticed Lena giving her a searching look. The tablets explained why Ariane Wirt seemed unusually calm and composed after everything that had happened, Lena reflected, nodding slowly.

'Suzanna was pretty much the best female swimmer in our group,' Lena recalled. 'She had all the trophies . . . Nobody else came close.'

Suzanna's mother's lips turned up slightly at the corners, and Lena was pleased to have brought a smile to her face.

'But you were always the braver one, don't you think?'

Lena looked through her for a moment. 'No, I don't think so. I think I just had a bigger mouth, that's all.' She cradled her chin in her hand, her arm resting on the table, and shook her head to herself. 'Something happened back then, and Suzanna and I – we were scared of getting into trouble, so we both promised never to tell a soul . . .' she started, sensing Wirt and Belling both looking at her. 'It was on a stormy Sunday afternoon . . . Despite the storm, Suzanna and I really wanted to swim out to the buoy . . . Then Suzanna stopped at the shore and decided against it after all, whereas I was being pig-headed about it and was already in the water. I didn't think about it, I just started swimming, and I was swimming away, struggling against the massive waves, being dragged further and further from the shore . . .'

Ariane Wirt stood up to take the whistling kettle off the hob, without taking her eyes off Lena.

'I can't have felt the exhaustion or the cold,' Lena continued hesitantly. 'But in the final metres before I got to the buoy, that's when it happened . . .' She gulped and took a deep breath. 'I suddenly got this terrible cramp. I screamed and was frantically splashing with my arms, but the waves just kept beating against me. And before I knew it, I had lost my bearings. I completely panicked and was using every last bit of strength to somehow keep myself afloat . . .' Lena paused a second and shook her head again. 'If it wasn't for Suzanna coming to help me . . .' She looked at Wirt. 'Your daughter saved my life that day.'

Silence fell over the room.

'Thank you for telling me that.' Ariane Wirt broke the silence. 'That means a lot to me.'

Lena nodded and glimpsed a surprised look on Wulf Belling's face, as though after hearing this story he finally understood why it was so important to her to solve this case.

He cleared his throat, then asked Frau Wirt: 'How long have you lived in Berlin?'

She ran her index finger over the bridge of her nose and thought. 'It's more than ten years. My husband was transferred here,' she said in a shaky voice, and Lena noticed her hands trembling as she poured the tea. 'In fact Suzanna and I have been living here alone most of the time. As I already told Lena on the phone, Konrad divorced me just a few months after we moved to Berlin.' With her lips pressed together, she put the kettle back on the hob. 'He never admitted it, but if you ask me, there was someone else in the picture.'

Belling looked up, startled, but said nothing.

Frau Wirt shook her head. 'Never mind – Suzanna and I coped perfectly well without him.' She put a steaming teacup down in front of Lena. With no milk.

'Thanks,' Lena said, maintaining her friendly smile. 'What kind of people did Suzanna associate with?'

Ariane Wirt sat down at the end of the table, at a right angle to where Lena and Belling were sitting. 'I've no idea.'

Lena's and Belling's eyes met. 'How had Suzanna been recently?' Lena asked. 'It's so long since I last saw her.'

She saw Suzanna's mother considering the question. 'Well, normal, I'd say.'

'Did Suzanna have a boyfriend?' Belling chimed in. 'Or did she perhaps mention any acquaintances who she met online?'

Again, Ariane Wirt replied with a shrug. She seemed not to have the slightest idea about her daughter's life.

'Have you ever heard the name Ferdinand Roggendorf or Dark Armon?' he asked.

'No, who's that then?'

'Someone we know from an online chatroom,' Lena interrupted.

Ariane Wirt stood up to put the photo of Suzanna back on the windowsill. She stared absentmindedly out into the garden for a moment, before turning around and asking Lena, 'Do you still go back to Fischbach at all?'

'Me? . . . Uh, no.' The question caught Lena off guard. Just the idea of going anywhere near there made her shudder.

'And what about your sister?' asked Ariane Wirt. 'Has she also come to Berlin?'

'No,' replied Lena and casually stirred her tea, though her feeling of discomfort grew. Nevertheless, she thought it appropriate to lay her cards out on the table, after asking the same of Ariane Wirt.

'Tamara and I lived with different foster families after we lost our parents in the car accident.' As memories of the car crash involuntarily welled up within her, she had a sense of the kitchen becoming oppressively small. The walls seemed to close in on her, and Lena had to force herself to calm down and fight the reflex to dash to the bathroom and scrub her hands clean. Lena gripped her teacup in order to hold on to something. 'But that was a long time ago,' she said, more for herself. Registering Belling's surprised look, she sat up straighter on her chair and forced herself to push away the memory. She looked at Ariane Wirt. 'What happened to Suzanna has touched me very personally,' she said, coming back to the original subject. 'Believe me, it's as important for me that Suzanna's killer is brought to justice as it is for you. But since we cannot rule out the possibility that Suzanna knew her killer, we need to know more about Suzanna's day-to-day life and the circle of people around her.'

Suddenly Ariane Wirt walked over to the sink, turned on the tap and started washing up the rest of the dishes.

A classic displacement activity, Lena thought and looked again at Belling.

'Frau Wirt, Suzanna was murdered – and whoever did it must have known that she regularly went jogging through the fen meadows by the River Tegel,' Belling continued.

Ariane Wirt carried on washing the dishes. 'After we moved to Berlin, Suzanna had a hard time making friends,' she said, her back to them. 'She retreated more and more into herself, even more so recently – I never got to speak to my daughter any more.'

Belling nodded sympathetically.

'May we have a look at Suzanna's room?' asked Lena.

'I don't think that's a good idea.' When Ariane Wirt turned around, tears were streaming down her cheeks. She put the sponge down and shook her head vehemently. 'For now, everything remains as it is, and I don't want anyone going into her room.'

For a moment there was silence. Belling's mobile rang. Clearing his throat, he pulled the phone out from his jacket pocket. After glancing at the caller's number, he looked at Lena. 'Excuse me.' He took the call and walked with long strides towards the door.

Lena watched him for a moment and gave Ariane Wirt a polite smile when Belling was gone. 'Thank you for taking the time to talk to us.'

Frau Wirt's face took on a rueful expression. 'I wish I could help you.'

Lena just nodded. She felt at a loss. Shortly afterwards, Belling came back into the kitchen holding his phone to his ear.

'Yes, of course – thanks, I owe you one.' He ended the call and gave Lena a look that did not bode well. She realised immediately what had happened.

'If you think of anything, please do call me,' Lena stressed, and grabbed her handbag, which she had hung on the back of the chair.

'I will do,' promised Ariane Wirt, and she led Lena and Belling back to the door.

Lena gave her another friendly nod before she hurriedly followed Belling to the car.

37

About twenty minutes later, Neukölln, Berlin

'This used to be a soap factory, and I've heard there are still some of the old conveyor belts down on the lower floors,' said Wulf Belling, as they reached the top floor and emerged from the dilapidated stairwell of the abandoned industrial building, which was filled with the stench of pigeon droppings, rotten food and urine. Ahead of them stretched an unlit hall. Only here and there a few rays of evening sun squeezed through the cracks between the boards nailed over the windows.

'According to my former colleague, the corpse was found here this morning, at about ten. The results are still not back from the autopsy. The same applies to the forensic team's analysis of the prints.'

Lena followed the beam of her torch through the scattered beer cans and sheets of newspapers, lighting up the dark areas that were separated by thick stone walls. 'Did this former colleague of yours also mention who found the body?'

'A homeless guy who sleeps here occasionally,' said Belling. 'Apparently he thought it was another tramp who had taken his spot. But when he saw that she was naked – plus all the blood – that's when he realised something nasty had happened and he contacted the police.'

Lena nodded thoughtfully and carried on walking. 'Has the body been identified?'

Belling picked up a box of Marlboros. When he saw that it was empty, he tossed it back on the ground. Suddenly something flashed past Lena. Rats.

'As far as I know, it's a thirty-two-year-old called Mandy Heart,' Belling said.

Lena looked at him. 'Mandy Heart – that doesn't sound like it's her real name.'

'No, that's what I thought,' he said, fumbling in his jacket pockets for his cigarettes. It seemed he had left them in the car.

'She worked as a waitress at Delirium, a pricey club near the Kurfürstendamm. It's rumoured that they offer their wealthy guests a lot more than just overpriced drinks . . .'

'I see,' murmured Lena and shone her torch around her. Torn-down cables hung from the ceiling and the pungent smell was getting stronger. But there was still something else in the air. Lena could feel her stomach churning. It was the stench of death that she had so often encountered at crime scenes.

'It must have been over there,' said Belling as he went ahead. Lena followed him towards a room off to one side, whose doorframe was barricaded with police tape.

'Let me guess – she'd been tied up and had the usual cuts and bruises?'

'No idea. I don't know the details, I'm afraid,' he said, before he froze at the doorway. His torch lit up the room. 'Jesus Chris – it's a bloodbath! The bastard properly butchered this one . . .'

Looking in a second after him, Lena gulped down the bile that rose to her throat as she saw the room. She shooed a blowfly from her shoulder, stooped to climb in under the police tape and let the beam of her torch glide over the walls and floor. She crouched down to inspect every square inch of this blood-spattered room while trying to keep in mind how the woman must have suffered in this godforsaken place. It was as though she could literally feel her fear, the echo as she screamed for her life.

'How insane must you need to be to do something like this to another person?' groaned Belling.

'Even the mentally ill have their motives for what they do,' murmured Lena. Then she stood up and said, 'Whoever did this – it's not the guy we're after.'

'What?' Horrified, he shone his torch into her face.

Lena shielded her eyes with her hand against the light and gestured to the room with her chin. 'What we see here was completely uncontrolled,' she explained, again casting the torchlight over the room. 'The perpetrator of this attack launched himself indiscriminately at the victim and got into a frenzy. But the guy we're after doesn't act like that. He has learned to control himself and he always proceeds according to the same pattern: he takes only what he needs and leaves the rest behind. And that's likely to be the main reason why he still hasn't been caught.'

Belling shook his head in amazement and breathed out with a whistle. 'Are you sure?'

She nodded.

'So this is a red herring, then? You don't think there's any connection?' he asked sceptically.

'I think it's highly unlikely that it's related. The approach is too different for it to be a copycat, and if it's a rival perpetrator, there don't seem to be enough clues that would suggest a recognisable signature.'

Even as she spoke, Lena felt a swell of anger that they were making such slow progress with their investigation. Much too slow. A thousand unanswered questions whizzed around her head, and once again it seemed to her that the person who might possibly have had some answers was Dr Cornelia Dobelli. And if there was one person who could help her find Dobelli, then that was Lukas with his skills as a hacker. She in no way wanted him to be drawn into the matter, but all the same she began seriously considering asking him for help.

Lena bent down to slip through the narrow gap in the police tape and join Belling on the other side.

'I tell you – this city is full of sick freaks,' he muttered, and after one last look at the crime scene he walked back towards the stairwell. Lena followed him.

'What's the news on Roggendorf?' Belling asked as they walked down the rusty metal stairs together. 'Has Drescher got him shadowed?'

'Well, he said he would,' said Lena.

Belling grumbled something that she didn't hear. 'It's not what I've heard,' he said enigmatically.

'Oh? What have you heard?' She continued to walk down the steps.

'That Ferdinand Roggendorf is currently working on his PhD – and guess what his topic is . . .'

As they reached the bottom, Lena lingered on the last stair. 'What? Don't just torture me with having to guess.'

He wrinkled his forehead, grinning. 'It's only about the transplantation of organic substances and preservation methods in anatomical dissection.'

Lena's eyes widened. 'Transplantation and plastination.'

'I'm telling you, Roggendorf's our man, but you didn't want to listen to me,' said Belling as his mobile rang. 'It wouldn't surprise me if my informant finds out next that Roggendorf also knew your friend,' he growled, then took the call.

'Hi, what's up?'

Lena watched as his expression suddenly changed.

'Helena . . .' He put a finger in his other ear and screwed up his face. 'How? Can you still hear me? Helena? Are you still there? . . . What is that that's so loud? . . . Yes . . . No, . . . Yes, tonight – exactly . . . What?! . . . No, but . . . Helena? I can't hear you properly . . . Yes, OK, I'll wait a sec. Call me back.'

He looked at Lena. 'This woman is driving me insane!'

'But you're still meeting up with her later,' said Lena with a compassionate smile.

'Yes,' he admitted. After checking his watch, he added: 'But not until later this evening. Shall we go and have a beer first?'

Lena nodded. 'Absolutely.'

No sooner had she said this than his mobile rang again. 'Sorry, just a second.' He turned away with his phone to his ear. Lena went a few steps ahead.

'What – now?' she heard him say behind her. 'But it's not even eight – we agreed that you'd go to your book club tonight and then we'd meet at the pub afterwards . . .'

Although he had his back to her, Lena saw how his shoulders slumped.

'Another appointment . . . OK, I get it . . . Well, if you have to . . .' He snorted. 'This appointment must be terribly important, otherwise you'd hardly drop your book club and relegate me to the support act.'

After he had hung up, he threw Lena a dismayed look. 'She's probably meeting that cosmetic surgeon again. I can't believe she's fallen for a guy like that . . .'

Lena walked over to Belling and put a hand on his shoulder. 'Hey, don't let it get you down,' she said and smiled at him. 'Maybe you need to work a bit harder for her. After all, you've let things slip for a while – it isn't going to be easy to make up for it with just one or two nice evenings.'

He lowered his eyes and nodded meekly. 'You're probably right.' He looked up. 'I guess we haven't got time for our beer after all.'

'No worries, another time.' She laughed. 'I'll go for one on my own – I'm a big girl.'

The evening sun stung Lena's eyes as they walked out of the soap factory and onto the street, going their separate ways.

'Oh, Peters . . .' Belling called back to her, as she was getting on to her Vespa.

'Yes?'

'If you come across that guy again – you know, the drunk one from last time – then say hello from me and tell him I can't wait to see him again!'

Lena rolled her eyes. 'Will do,' she said, smiling. Belling's protective instinct was well intentioned, but she could take good care of herself.

38

Meanwhile in Berlin city centre

Carmen Martinez parked her bright red Golf in front of the little Italian restaurant in the Acker Strasse at exactly eight-thirty. La Trattoria was tucked between a cigar shop and a small hat shop and was well known for both its culinary specialties and its excellent wines. The chances of finding somewhere to park at this time of day right by the restaurant were about as high as winning the lottery, which Carmen took as a good omen. She sat in the car for a couple of minutes and peered over at the restaurant. She didn't want to be the first to arrive. Although she hardly knew the man whom she was supposed to be meeting exactly two minutes ago, she had a slight tingling feeling in her stomach for the first time since she had moved to Berlin from Dortmund a good three months ago for a traineeship at the law firm Seiberts & Partners. Carmen pulled down the sun visor and checked how she looked in the mirror. She had tied up her chestnut-brown hair and put on dark eye shadow. She was wearing a short pastel-coloured dress that she had bought especially for the occasion. It was really a bit too expensive, but after the shop assistant had convinced her that she looked a dress size 38 rather than the 44 she really was, she simply had to have it. Carmen hated feeling chubby, and yet she loved her food. And besides, she told herself, it was Martin Jung who had spoken to her first, not the other way around. Their first encounter last week, however, was a bit of a disaster. She had been impatiently waiting in the queue at City Coffee and had ordered a latte macchiato and a large piece of chocolate cake with whipped cream, when a table by the window became free. She had quickly handed the cashier the money and taken her tray, and was heading straight for the window seat when, in her hurry, she collided with a man. The chocolate cake slipped from the tray and landed on her lemon-yellow silk blouse, while the latte macchiato sprayed everywhere across the floor. It was carnage. Carmen turned as red as a lobster in front of everyone and wished she could just disappear into the ground. Although she was convinced it was her own clumsiness that was to blame, the attractive stranger absolutely insisted she let him pay for her blouse to be dry-cleaned. And he was adamant about buying her a new latte macchiato and piece of cake. Carmen did not need to be asked twice. And when she ran into him again, quite by chance, the next day at Hackescher Markt, not far from her office, she could hardly believe that he actually still remembered her. The man, who later introduced himself as Martin Jung, asked whether the chocolate stains had come out of her silk blouse. Carmen, who would never have dreamed of meeting this man again, simply smiled at him with sparkling eyes and nodded. In truth, she had thrown away the blouse – she'd always felt it made her look even chubbier than she already was. Carmen first of all thought he was joking when the stranger invited her to go for a coffee. But his face suggested the opposite. There was nothing she would have liked more than to accept his invitation, but unfortunately she had already had her lunch break and with all the will in the world she couldn't afford to annoy her new boss at the law firm. So she had to decline Martin Jung's invitation. However, luck was clearly on her side because the coffee invitation was promptly upgraded to an invitation to dinner. Carmen knew she was no beauty, so it was all the more flattering that this attractive stranger had asked her out on a date.

The rest of the week had passed by infinitely slowly and Carmen had been counting the days until this evening. Excited, she now sat behind the wheel of her car and powdered her nose. When she closed the sun visor again, there was a smile plastered across her face. Another spritz of perfume here and there, and then, with her heart pounding, she got out of the car. A moment or two later, she stepped into the restaurant.

'*Buona sera, signorina*,' she was greeted by a waiter as he rushed by. 'Do you have a reservation?'

Carmen nodded shyly and let her gaze wander through the restaurant, which was packed to the very last seat. Besides the display cabinet showing the various antipasti dishes, she looked at the fifteen tables that each had a candle on them, giving the room a warm, cosy atmosphere.

'Yes – that is, no . . . The reservation isn't in my name, but . . .' She looked around helplessly and had almost resigned herself to the fact that he had changed his mind, when she spotted him at a table tucked away at the back of the restaurant. Carmen stuck her arm in the air and waved enthusiastically. Martin Jung discreetly raised his hand. He smiled at her, then lowered his gaze back to the menu. Instead of the jacket he was wearing at their unfortunate first encounter at City Coffee, he had chosen a dark shirt for the occasion. His blond hair was not parted this time, but combed back.

He's even more attractive than I remembered, thought Carmen, as the waiter led her over to the table.

The evening went exactly as Carmen might have hoped. Martin Jung was funny, intelligent and far more charismatic than any of the men she'd had anything to do with so far. He wasn't sparing with his compliments, particularly about her nose, even if Carmen could not for the life of her understand what it was about it that he found so special. They laughed a lot together and even came so close at one point that their faces were almost touching. And as they were eating their dessert, Martin Jung put the cherry on the cake when he told her that he owned a junk shop. She had such a penchant for antiques and retro furniture! As far as she was concerned, this evening could go on for ever.

39

When the young woman disappeared to the toilet, Artifex stared in her direction. While he had been convinced that the petite reporter was a one-off lucky strike, he now wondered if he had to revise this assessment. Throughout the evening, he had considered Carmen's nose in detail and had come to the decision that Tilla would be as delighted by it as by the lips of Svenja Stollberg. Meanwhile, Carmen Martinez was new in town and, over the course of the entire evening, had not mentioned a boyfriend or any other friends or acquaintances. This suggested that there was no one who would be out looking for her straight away. Now all he had to do was to convince her to leave her car and to go with him, and then everything would go exactly according to plan. Somehow he rather liked the plump young woman, although that would not alter the fact that he had to kill her. Just like the others, she was nothing more to him than an object, an element of his artistic creation. Martinez's nose was an almost perfect fit and it was one of the few ingredients that he was still missing. It would be just a few more days, perhaps another week or two, and then he would finally be able to complete his masterpiece. Tilla would be so proud of him. For a while Artifex thought about granting Martinez one last favour and actually showing her around his junk shop. It was all the same to him where he did it. However, he would have to be careful not to leave any bloodstains in the shop. After all, on paper it was still Tilla's shop and he didn't want to annoy her in the slightest.

When Carmen Martinez came back to the table, Artifex noticed that she had powdered her little pointy nose. He had to smile inwardly. *You could have saved yourself the effort . . .*

'Shall we?' she asked, smiling at him expectantly.

'Sure.' He pushed back his chair and gallantly offered her his arm to hook hers into as, with a smirk on his lips, he led his next victim out of the restaurant.

40

At the same time, a few streets away

At about 10 p.m., Lena parked her scooter outside the Kings Club. Posters for 'The Preachers' were plastered on the wall next to the entrance to the club, which was located under an S-Bahn railway bridge. Lena looked forward to seeing Lukas again. Not least because he represented her only real chance of tracking down Dr Dobelli. There was quite a long queue at the door, but as Lena was on the guest list, she was let in straight away. Inside, the club was packed. It was hot and stuffy, and a mix of punk rock and heavy metal boomed out of the speakers. Lena did not have to look hard before she spotted Lukas. He was on stage, playing the drums, and he seemed absolutely in his element. She watched him for a while. She could hardly suppress a little smile. Somehow, she had always had a soft spot for musicians. Then she tore her gaze away from him, got herself a gin and tonic at the bar and joined the crowd on the dance floor. It was no later than the second drink that she started to feel the tension of the day unravelling. Lena let herself be carried along with the ecstatic mass, but still kept one eye on Lukas. When the band took a break some time later, Lena weaved her way quickly through the crowd towards Lukas and caught up with him just in front of the stage. He seemed visibly surprised to see her – he had obviously not really expected her to come.

'Well, look here – the later it gets, the more interesting the guests!' he shouted against the loud music, which echoed through the club.

Lena could barely hear him, but smiled and held her empty glass in the air. 'What do you think? Shall we get another drink?'

Lukas gestured with a nod for her to follow him to the bar. They found two free bar stools and ordered some drinks. It was much quieter over there. Lena congratulated him on the successful gig.

'Thank you – even if you missed the best part!'

'What was that?' Lena asked.

'Well, my drum solo at the start,' he said jokingly, and laughed.

Lena smiled sheepishly. Mainly because she did not know what else to say, she quickly brought up the matter of needing to pinpoint Dr Dobelli's whereabouts.

Lukas moved his bar stool closer to hers. 'So this address is pretty important to you, right?'

Lena just nodded and clinked glasses with him when their drinks were served.

'What do you want from this Dr Whatsit anyway?' Lukas asked.

'Is that important?'

'It obviously is to you.'

She looked down at her drink. Then she pulled out a pen, scribbled the name *Dr Cornelia Dobelli* on a beer mat and pushed it over to Lukas.

He glanced at the name then pocketed the beer mat. 'I'll see what I can do,' he said with a wink.

Lena smiled at him gratefully. *Very good.*

They chatted for a while about this and that, and as Lena emptied another glass, she felt that she had already drunk more than she would have liked. It was time to go. Lena stood up and was just about to say goodbye when Lukas pulled her in close.

'If I get you this address, you owe me one . . .'

Lena had difficulty withstanding his gaze. 'Till then,' she said quickly, looking into the distance.

41

It was already well past midnight when Lena turned her Vespa into Boxhagener Strasse. It was only now, when she was nearly home, that she realised how much she had been zigzagging about. Lena slowed down to a stop, got off her scooter and told herself to be much more restrained the next time she was out having a drink. She took off her helmet and pushed the scooter through the unlit courtyard, thinking about Belling's date with his ex-wife. If she was honest with herself, she had had a slightly uneasy feeling since she first met him. Lena locked up the scooter and could not make sense of how it was that Belling had been sitting at the same bar as her, drowning his sorrows in a glass of vodka on ice, when she felt her mobile phone ringing in her bag. Lena had to smile. What was that, if not telepathy? She hastily rummaged through her bag for her phone. Large handbags and small mobile phones were an unbelievably bad combination, she thought to herself.

'Lena Peters speaking.' She tried to talk softly so as not to wake the neighbours.

'Good evening, my little Lena . . .' The caller's voice sounded strangely distorted.

With her phone at her ear, Lena stopped in the middle on the yard. 'Who's this?'

'Today must be your lucky day, little Lena – I'm the one you've been looking for all this time . . .'

She heard a short burst of laughter at the other end the line.

'Did you seriously believe that amateurish mess at the old soap factory was my work? Pah! You disappoint me, little Lena.'

Lena froze. An icy shiver ran down her spine when she realised who she was speaking to. She sobered up instantly as she looked around the dark courtyard. No sign of anyone or anything.

'No, I didn't,' she replied, trying to speak in a neutral tone, while at the same time wondering how on earth he could know that she and Belling had been to the disused soap factory.

'Good girl.'

'Who are you?'

'My name is Artifex. The "Mutilator" is such an ugly name for what I'm doing,' said the unfamiliar voice.

Lena urged herself to remain calm, while she felt her heart racing. 'How do I know you're actually who you're claiming to be?'

Again there came a smug laugh. 'There are no guarantees in life. There is only death . . . And you, my little Lena, are playing with fire. And you know what fire can do, don't you?'

Lena flinched and felt her forehead burning. 'I don't know what you're talking about. Explain it to me,' she said with a dry mouth, determined to keep him on the line to learn as much as possible about his personality.

The voice laughed again. 'Oh yes, my dear Lena, you know very well. 'And then the voice asked her: 'Do you still have the smell of burned skin in your nose, little Lena?'

This was clearly a reference to her parents' car accident. Lena had the sensation of the ground under her feet falling away. *Stay calm, concentrate!*

'How do you know about the accident?' As difficult as it was for her, she did her best to sound composed.

'Maybe there are more parallels between us than you would like there to be . . . Believe me, little Lena – I know full well what it feels like to grow up without any parents.'

'How did you know about my parents' car accident?' she asked again.

But her question would remain unanswered.

The line was already dead.

42

Weak in the knees, Lena stumbled to her door and nervously dialled Wulf Belling's number. She heard the dial tone, but there was no answer. *Come on, pick up!* Lena tried again, but to no avail. She was still recovering from the shock when, all of a sudden, a figure stepped out of the darkness. Lena jumped back in terror and instinctively ducked to shield herself.

'Hello, Lena.'

'Jesus!' She breathed out heavily and slapped the palm of her hand against her chest in relief when she saw Tamara in the pale moonlight.

'Why so jumpy? That's not like you, sis.'

Baffled, Lena stared at her for a second, speechless. 'What are you doing here?' Although still shaken by the phone call, she wondered for a moment what was more of a shock: a phone call from a serial killer or her twin sister turning up out of the blue – after years of silence, all of a sudden standing here on her doorstep with a suitcase.

Tamara grinned. 'This is how you welcome your only sister?'

Lena made every effort to conceal her tension. 'Where have you come from?'

Tamara shrugged and sighed. 'From everywhere and nowhere.'

'And how long have you been standing there?'

'I don't know, not very long. I saw the light on and thought you were at home.' She laughed mockingly. 'But apparently you still the leave the light on when you go out, huh?'

Lena swallowed down the response that was on the tip of her tongue. She was amazed when Tamara stepped closer and in the moonlight she saw a baby wrapped in a blanket in her sister's arms. Lena quickly unlocked the door and let Tamara and the baby into the flat. Tamara was wearing a short denim skirt and a midriff-baring yellow top that could have come from Rebecca Brandt's wardrobe. She had just a thin jacket on over it. Her shoulder-length hair was matted and she looked even more of a mess that Lena remembered.

'It's a boy. His name's Marcel,' said Tamara proudly.

'A beautiful name,' said Lena, looking lovingly at the little thing before she looked up at her sister. 'Tamara, I'm so sorry, but you can't—'

'Want to hold him a second?' Tamara interrupted and gently handed her the infant. No sooner did Lena have the baby in her arms than she felt the enormous tension briefly subside a little and a warm feeling run through her. She gazed at the tiny hands. The angelic face. Everything about him was so fragile and vulnerable. She stroked his head tenderly, his soft baby hair. Blinking, the little creature gradually opened his sleepy eyes. He smiled at Lena and started wriggling under his blanket. He was a sweet little thing and Lena immediately opened up her heart to him. Children had this effect on her and it had always been her dream to start her own family one day. With at least two or three children. But fate had provided a different life for her. And the sad truth was that her job hardly ever brought her into contact with children. And if it did, they weren't alive.

'I was fed up and thought I'd come and see what's so great about Berlin,' said Tamara, pushing her fringe out of her eyes with an uncontrolled movement. 'I chucked in my job at the laundry – my boss was an asshole.'

Lena stared at her in silence and lowered her eyes back to the baby.

'No need to look like that. I'll find something else. You know me . . .' Tamara said, leaning against the front door with her arms folded.

'And what's that?' asked Lena with a reproachful glance at the blue-green bruise on Tamara's forehead, which had been covered up by her fringe until then. 'Did you forget what I had to do to defend you from guys like that?'

'What? I fell down the stairs. It's what you get if you don't look where you're going.'

Lena just glared at her angrily.

'All right, you win,' said Tamara, defeated, as she smoothed her fringe down in the hallway wardrobe's mirror. 'What am I supposed to do? These bastards don't have a sign on their foreheads saying whether they beat women up or not. But, believe me, I've had it with guys like that.'

Exactly what you've said every time, thought Lena, suppressing a sigh. Somehow she did feel sorry for her sister. 'And where have you left Fabienne?' Fabienne was Tamara's eight-year-old daughter. As Tamara had been intimate with several men before she got pregnant, it was unclear who the girl's father was. And given that none of the men had 'anything to offer', she had not bothered carrying out a paternity test. So Lena saved herself the trouble of asking who little Marcel's father was.

'She's with a friend of mine.'

'Which friend?' Lena sounded suspicious even to her own ears.

Defiantly, Tamara looked at her hands. 'You don't know her.'

Lena did not believe a word. 'Please don't tell me you've left Fabienne with Cindy again.'

'Why not? Cindy's been clean for four months now.'

'Oh yes? Did Cindy tell you that? And what if she was lying again?' Lena exclaimed, louder than she intended. She told herself to keep it down, so as not to frighten little Marcel, who had fallen asleep in her arms.

Tamara made a face. 'My friends have never been good enough for you.' Angrily, she took the child out of Lena's arms. 'But unlike you, sis, at least I have some.'

Shaking her head, Lena crossed her arms. 'Oh congratulations – so nothing's changed! I cannot understand how you can leave your child in the care of a junkie.'

'Ex-junkie,' said Tamara, rolling her eyes. 'Oh, man . . . Cindy is taking my daughter to school every day and to homework club and everything. The whole shebang.' She twisted her lips into a thin smile. 'It's all taken care of.'

Lena was silent, thinking what to say. 'Tamara, listen, you really can't stay here,' she continued. They were not easy words to say. And even if her instinct told her that the Mutilator was not going to just show up at her house, the last thing she wanted was to bring Tamara and the baby into any kind of danger.

'Oh yeah?' Tamara gave her an annoyed look. 'And may I ask why not?'

'I'm working on a case and—' Lena bit her tongue. 'Just believe me – I can't tell you right now.'

'That's just typical!' Tamara exclaimed with contempt. 'You're *sooo* important!' The little one in her arms began to scream. 'Tsh, so where am I supposed to go?'

Instead of replying, Lena pulled out her mobile and phoned a few hotels to see if anywhere had a free room. She finally got lucky at Smith's, an upmarket hotel in Prenzlauer Berg. Lena reserved a single room with a cot. Then she called for a taxi. Tamara stood there in front of her the whole time, looking indignant.

'Here,' said Lena, pulling out her purse and handing Tamara eighty euros.

Tamara stared at the money. 'That's it?'

Lena checked through the rest of her change and pressed the remaining euro coins into Tamara's hand. 'I'll have found another solution by tomorrow, OK?' She tried to smile, hoping that Tamara would not make any more fuss and would agree.

Tamara pouted, but pocketed the money and picked up her bag. It pained Lena to see her sister turn and go with the screaming baby. Tamara was almost out the door when she stood on the doorstep and turned to Lena.

'It's because of the baby, right? You can't bear the sight of him, because Mother Nature foiled your plans and you know you're never going to have your own.'

That was too much. Lena shook her head and closed the door without a reply. She leaned back against the wall and took several deep breaths to calm herself down. First the phone call, then Tamara. Lena tried to get her thoughts into some meaningful order. But she felt as if she was being buried.

43

A few hours later

Lena felt fuzzy as she sat up in bed and pushed her hair off her sweaty forehead. Yet again the memory of her parents' burning car had crept into her dreams. Help came too late for her parents. It was now nearly two decades since the accident, but every now and then Lena still pictured the blood on her hands. It was the kind of dream that felt so horribly real that even after waking she still felt anxious. This time, her dream had not ended with her mother's bloody hand but with the phone call from the killer. She was still deeply shaken by it. Lena stared at the dark bedroom ceiling, going over and over his words in her head. The same questions kept coming back to her: What prompted Artifex to call her? How did he get her number? And how did he know about her past?

Lena was wide awake when she got out of bed and heard Napoleon meowing as he sat on the patio by the door. She let the cat in and was walking sleepily to the kitchen when she saw a dummy on the hallway floor near the front door. She picked it up and could not help thinking about little Marcel. As she pictured his big wide eyes, which had beamed at her so heartbreakingly, a wistful smile appeared on Lena's lips. She wondered where Tamara and the baby were right now. In the best scenario, they would be in the hotel, but with Tamara you never knew for sure. It would not have surprised Lena if she had spent the money long before she even got to the hotel. Lena was frequently exasperated by her sister's irresponsibility. When she reached the kitchen, Lena took an aspirin for her headache and washed it down with a sip of water, as her gaze turned to the photos of the dead women on the fridge. Might the killer have called them before their deaths? This phone call seemed to be completely new behaviour for him and did not quite seem to fit the image that Lena had of the psychopath in her head. Though a serial killer making contact with an investigator might not feel out of place in Hollywood, in reality it was highly unusual. Especially as Lena was officially off the case. She poured herself a glass of water and thought feverishly about what kind of thought process this Artifex was following and what he wanted to achieve by phoning her. But in her mind there was nothing but a blank space. She took out her mobile and tried to call Wulf Belling, after she had tried umpteen times to contact him last night. Yet again, she did not get through. She drank the water and strolled back to her bedroom. Napoleon came towards her, mewing from the door to the living room. Lena stooped and stroked his dappled coat. Just to eat and sleep and a little stroke here and there – *that's the life*, she thought, as she spontaneously glanced over at the game of chess on the chest of drawers. Without thinking, Lena went over to the chessboard and moved the black queen two spaces forwards.

'Checkmate!' she said with pleasure and wondered how she could have missed that all this time.

Sometimes the answer is so close that you miss it, thought Lena and went back to bed.

44

Meanwhile at Rebecca Brandt's flat, Wilmersdorf, Berlin

The click of handcuffs and a faint giggle could be heard in the candle-lit hallway, where black nylon stockings, knickers and a lace bra lay scattered across the floor. The door to the bedroom was open. On the windowsill glowed a kitsch red and purple lava lamp. In the middle of the darkly furnished room stood a large metal bed. Rebecca Brandt lay on her back, her hands cuffed to the iron bedstead. Her eyes were blindfolded with a black velvet ribbon. Her legs were wrapped around Volker Drescher. A moan escaped her throat while Drescher caressed her firm breasts with his tongue, slowly working up towards her neck. Drescher groped with one hand for the condom that lay between their work mobiles and his glasses on the bedside table. He took a corner of the packet between his teeth and was about to rip it open when one of the phones rang. Drescher sat up with a sigh. A glance at the screen told him that the call was from the office.

Groaning, Brandt sank into the pillow. 'Don't stop ... not now...'

Drescher's eyes moved indecisively back and forth between Rebecca Brandt and the ringing mobile phone. 'It could be important.'

'Oh, they can manage one night without you.'

Shortly afterwards, the ringing stopped.

'You see, it probably wasn't that important . . .' whispered Brandt with a seductive smile, her eyes still blindfolded. She raised her head and ran her tongue over his lips. Drescher let his eyes wander over her flawless naked body.

'Where we were, then?' he asked with a grin, when a loud beep announced the arrival of a text message.

'I'm sorry, but I can't ignore it.' He sat up, grabbed his glasses from the bedside table and picked up the phone. Suddenly he burst out laughing.

'What's so funny?'

'It's your phone,' he said, amused, 'and I see it's from Charlie. Since when have you been texting our archivist?'

Brandt frantically tried to sit up. 'Please put it back!'

Drescher had no intention of doing so. He held the phone in the air and had fun watching her try to grab it. But the laughter stopped when his eyes caught sight of the message. Then he looked at Rebecca Brandt, aghast.

'I don't believe it – so that's what happened!' He tore the blindfold from her eyes.

'Uh, what?' She blinked at him in surprise.

'I cannot believe it!' Enraged, he beat his hand against the bedstead.

'What . . . what are you talking about?' stammered Brandt.

'Don't pretend you don't know – Dr Dobelli's file, of course!' He gave Rebecca Brandt a disappointed look before he went to gather up his clothes from the floor.

'No need to fly off the handle,' said Brandt, trying to appease him. Drescher paid no attention. He slipped into his trousers and his leather shoes, pulled his shirt on over his head and buttoned it up quickly.

'When did you say your cleaning lady comes?'

'Tomorrow morning. Why?' she asked, confused.

'Does she have a key?'

'Yes, but what's with all the questions?'

Without another word, Drescher grabbed his jacket and headed for the door.

'Hey, haven't you forgotten something?' Rebecca Brandt shouted after him and rattled her handcuffs on the bedstead.

Suddenly Drescher stopped in the doorway and walked back over to her. 'Oh, right.' He picked up his phone from the bedside table and turned around again.

Brandt stared after him, aghast. 'Hey! What are you doing? Let me go!'

Drescher put the keys to the handcuffs on the dresser by the door. 'Tell that to your cleaning lady, who's used to cleaning up your mess.'

'Hey! You cannot do this! COME BACK!'

Drescher slammed the door to her apartment behind him.

45

The semi-detached house where Wulf Belling lived was in a busy street near Friedenau S-Bahn station. It was not one of the most attractive houses in the road, but Belling felt very comfortable there, although they were a bit short on domestic bliss these days. His daughter's furious voice could be heard out in the street.

'You're calling me a liar?!' Marietta screamed from her room.

'And what do you call this?' Wulf Belling was in the hall, holding a bag of marijuana in the air.

'I cannot believe you've searched my room!' She yanked at her plum-coloured severely cut short hair, while stamping back and forth in her room.

'What was I supposed to do? You never tell me anything!' he countered and put the bag in his pocket.

Marietta's narrowed her black kohl-lined eyes. 'For God's sake, Dad, that stuff is ancient! I've told you, I haven't touched the stuff for ages – or anything else!' Her disappointment about his mistrust was clear to see on her face.

Belling was just about to say something when his mobile rang on the dresser. He could see that it was Lena Peters. She had already tried to call him several times, but after meeting Helena the night before he had not had the slightest desire to communicate with another human being. He now decided to take the call.

'Yes, Belling here ... What? Jesus Christ!' he blurted out in horror. He looked at his watch and nodded. 'In twenty minutes. OK, see you soon,' he said, hanging up.

'What? One phone call and the conversation's over – just like that?' shouted Marietta, who lay on her bed sulking, watching through the open door as he pulled on his jacket. 'You've got nothing else to say?'

Belling grabbed his car keys from the dresser and looked guiltily at his daughter. 'Listen, we'll talk later, OK?'

Angrily, his daughter hurled a cushion at him. 'You don't give a shit about me – just like Mum!'

'Marietta, you know that's not true! Besides—' But before he could finish the sentence, she had already jumped off the bed and slammed the door in his face.

'Damn it!' Belling stamped his foot furiously. He had already lost his wife and now he was about to screw things up with his daughter too. He knocked on her bedroom door. 'Oh, please, Jetta, come on.'

'How many times have I told you – do *not* call me Jetta!' he heard through the door, just as she turned up the volume on the heavy metal. Depressed, Belling stared for a moment at the bedroom door. He raised his hand to knock on the door again, but then let it fall, resigned to the futility of the situation.

Not a lot I can do, he said to himself and left the house.

46

Bacon 'n' Cheese was on a street corner halfway between Friedrichshain and Friedenau and was one of the few cafes in the area that opened early in the morning. The interior was simple and unpretentious, possibly the reason why it was still largely devoid of tourists. It was still very quiet and Lena had chosen a table by the window, from where she could keep an eye on the door. She poked at her eggs on toast without much of an appetite, looking impatiently at the clock. It was already twenty to nine – Belling should be coming any minute now. She ordered another espresso from the waitress as she hurried past and gazed back at the door. Just as two men left with a pug dog on a lead, Wulf Belling stepped in the door. When he saw Lena, he headed straight towards her. She noticed that he was wearing the scruffy jacket again instead of his new corduroy one, from which she concluded that his date with his ex-wife had not gone well.

'Thanks for coming,' said Lena with a tense smile.

Belling hung his jacket over the back of his chair and sat down. He looked miserable. And exhausted, as though he had spent last night peering at the bottom of his glass.

'Are you kidding? I mean, damn – last night you had a phone call from—' He fell silent when the waitress stopped by their table and served Lena her espresso.

'What can I get you?' she asked Belling.

He squinted at Lena's plate. 'Bring me the same and a double espresso. Oh, and extra bacon with the eggs, please.'

The waitress took his order and disappeared. Belling asked, 'Have you any idea why this – what did you say he called himself?'

'Artifex.'

'Why this Artifex called you in particular?' he continued in a low voice.

Lena shook her head and, contemplatively swirling the espresso cup in her hand, she went over the conversation again word for word. She lifted the cup to put it to her mouth, and then put it down again the next second.

'There's something else,' she added hesitantly. Unintentionally, her voice betrayed a hint of vulnerability as she said: 'He knew about my parents' car accident.'

The horror was stark in Belling's face. 'How the hell did he know about that?' He sounded gravely concerned.

Lena looked up from her cup. 'I have no idea,' she sighed. 'All I know is that I'm about to board a plane to Edinburgh, to go and visit Dr Cornelia Dobelli at the care home.'

Belling was confused. 'Care home? Edinburgh? Huh?' He scratched his head. 'What on earth has led you there?'

Lena began to tell him, and Belling remained astonished as she described Lukas and his impressive skills as a hacker. Then she pulled out a piece of paper with the address of Eastfield House, a mental health care home, which Lukas had pushed under her apartment door.

Belling looked at it, perplexed. 'It says Dr Dobelli is there as a patient?'

Lena nodded.

'I don't know – something about it seems a bit odd to me,' he muttered, throwing Lena a suspicious look. 'Are you sure you can trust this Lukas?'

'Nope.' But her gut feeling told her the opposite. 'But I probably have very little choice, right?'

'Have you checked whether Dr Dobelli is actually a resident?'

Lena pensively stirred her coffee. 'Of course,' she said, looking up. 'But as you can imagine, the staff in psychiatric facilities are not keen to disclose information about patients.'

That made sense to Belling. 'Patient confidentiality,' he added with a sigh.

Again Lena nodded. 'And unfortunately my contacts don't quite reach as far as Scotland.' She took out her notebook and wrote down the address of the care home. Then she pushed the scrap of paper over the table to Belling. 'I want you to keep that. If I'm not back in two days, then . . .'

'Got it.' He popped the note into his jacket pocket. Then he lit a cigarette between his lips just as the waitress brought over his double espresso and eggs on toast.

'Sorry, no smoking in here.' She made no attempt to mask her annoyed tone of voice.

'Yeah . . . right,' groaned Belling and reluctantly put the cigarette away again. He was just about to launch into his eggs when he suddenly called the waitress back.

'Hi, uh, miss.'

'Something wrong?' sighed the waitress when she was back at their table.

'My bacon – you forgot my bacon.' A despondent shrug.

With a sullen expression, she took the plate away. Belling gave her a frugal smile. 'Thanks.' He leaned back in his chair, his arms folded, and looked at the waitress, sunk in thought. 'Tsk . . . Helena never forgot my bacon . . .'

'So how did it go yesterday?' Lena asked gently.

Belling looked at her, as if the question was a painful one. He sat slumped in his chair and shook his head expressively. 'To put it politely: awful,' he groaned and made a defensive gesture, making it clear that he did not want to talk about it.

Lena nodded and had enough tact not to grill him any more. 'There's something else I wanted to ask you about,' she mentioned instead, in a meek tone.

'And that would be?'

Lena told him about Tamara suddenly appearing out of the blue in the middle of the night at her door. 'I really have no idea where I can accommodate her and the baby,' she said helplessly. 'All I know is that I don't want to expose her to any risk by having her close to me.'

'I see . . .' He dropped two sugar cubes into his espresso. 'What about if I put your sister and the baby up with me initially?' he suggested and sat up in his chair. 'Just until she gets herself set up, of course.'

Astonished, Lena smiled. 'With you?'

'Why not? It wouldn't hurt to bring a little life back to the place. Since Helena's been gone, it's been pretty quiet around the house.'

Lena was sceptical. 'And your daughter?'

'Marietta is almost never at home. And anyway, even when we do see each other, we don't have much to say to each other.' He folded his hands on the table. 'No, don't worry about it. Besides, there's plenty of space in the house.'

But Lena was unsure whether she could really ask him to take on Tamara. But her objections were met with deaf ears.

'Your twin sister can hardly be worse than Marietta.'

She stared at him anxiously. He really had no idea. But since she could not think of a better solution for the time being, she finally gave in.

Once the waitress had brought him his eggs and toast – this time with extra bacon – Belling pounced on it, as though it was an eternity since he last had a hot meal.

Lena pushed her plate aside and drank her espresso.

'Are you not going to have that?' he asked.

She smirked. 'Help yourself.'

He did not need to be told twice and pulled the plate over to him. After another look at her watch, Lena asked for the bill.

When Belling had devoured her leftovers, he placed his knife and fork on his plate and looked at her indecisively for a few seconds. 'Can you shoot?' he asked and dabbed his mouth with his serviette.

The question surprised Lena. 'Depends what you mean . . . I took a course once, but that was ages ago. Why do you ask?'

After a quick glance over his shoulders, Belling stuck his hand in his jacket pocket and pulled out something that was wrapped in a cloth. He passed it to her across the table.

Lena realised at once what it was.

'Take it,' he whispered to her.

'Listen, I can look after myself without this,' she said in a hushed voice.

'Take it – just in case. This guy is dangerous. He already has your number. What if he turns up at your door next?'

Lena felt her stomach clench at the thought. 'I don't know. All who take up the sword will perish by the sword – that's what the Bible says.'

'But Jesus didn't have a psychotic serial killer after him! I'm not saying take it with you to Scotland. But do me a favour and at least put the damn thing under your pillow or something.'

Lena still hesitated. She cast a nervous glance at the counter, where the waitress was totting up their bill. When she saw the young woman heading in her direction, Lena quickly pushed her chair back and placed the pistol unceremoniously into her handbag. Wulf Belling looked visibly relieved. The waitress left the bill on the table and Lena was just about to pull out her purse when Belling beat her to it.

'This is on me.'

'No, no way.'

But Belling insisted. Lena smiled and put her purse back. 'Thanks.'

'Meanwhile, I'll keep an eye on Roggendorf,' Belling suggested when the waitress was out of earshot.

Lena nodded. 'Oh, and you might also want to have a word with the colleagues of Suzanna Wirt? Perhaps they might know something.'

'Will do.' Belling looked at her. 'And Lena . . .'

'Yes?'

'Take care of yourself.'

She smiled. Then she left the cafe.

47

The same time, Schöneberg, Berlin

Gemmy lay on the old mattress in the back room of the junk shop, staring mesmerised at the screen while his fingers raced madly about on the PlayStation controller. After having to surrender to an armada of zombies for the third time in a row, he lost interest. All that killing had worked up an appetite, even if it was only in his virtual first-person shooter world. Gemmy put the controller aside, dragged himself up and sauntered into the tiny kitchenette on the lookout for something to eat. On the shelf he found only empty biscuit tins. The cupboard above the sink had nothing more to offer. He glanced in the fridge where there was just half a pizza, which had a layer of greenish-blue mould growing on it. He had more luck in the icebox: a frozen lasagne and a box of ice cream. He licked his lips and then, a moment later, he discovered something else. There was something wrapped in a freezer bag. He took the bag out and held it in the air with one hand.

'Oh, man, that's gross!' When he realised that the rubbery-looking object was a human nose, his appetite instantly vanished. 'Holy shit!' Disgusted, he lowered his arm with the bag in his hand. 'Shit, man – and I thought it was all talk from that nutter,' Gemmy blurted out, as shocked as he was intrigued, when suddenly he heard someone coming in the shop door. Startled, he turned around and, quick as a flash, shoved everything back in the freezer. Then he hurried into the back room to switch off the TV and the PlayStation and climbed into the rickety wardrobe to hide. After the gruesome discovery in the icebox he thought it wiser not to let Artifex know that he had had a duplicate key made so he could hang out at the junk shop in his absence. Gemmy held his breath when he saw through the slats of the wardrobe door that Artifex had entered the back room. He was holding a container of chemicals in each hand, which he placed into a large cardboard box together with a cord, a tarpaulin, several hoses and freezer bags. Gemmy was sweating profusely as he watched Artifex pack saws of various sizes into the box before he picked it up to take with him. Driven by an irrepressible curiosity, he slipped out of the wardrobe and followed Artifex at a safe distance out to the black van, which was parked outside the junk shop. Hiding behind the dustbins, he watched as Artifex left the box in the van, then went back into the shop and returned shortly after with another one. Gemmy burned with curiosity to know what he was up to. And as Artifex disappeared once more into the shop, he took the opportunity to creep into the back of the van. He grabbed an old blanket and hid behind one of the boxes towards the back. A short while later, he heard the rear doors of the van being closed and the engine starting up with a loud rattle.

48

Lena tucked the gun into one of the drawers in her bedroom chest. A glance at the clock told her that she was already running late. She quickly tossed a few more things into her travel bag. She was packing a few extra things just in case, as she had no way of knowing how long she would be in Edinburgh. She had just pulled the zip shut on her bag when her phone rang. Lena flinched. To her relief, the screen did not show an unknown number, but Volker Drescher's. As she had already seen from the missed calls list, Drescher had tried to reach her several times over the past few days. Although she was well aware that she should inform Drescher about the phone call from the killer, she made no attempt to answer. Too great was her mistrust of him after everything that happened. Her mobile phone was not silent for long; the landline started ringing in the hall. Lena just shook her head with a sigh and ignored the ringing. As she was carrying her bag into the hallway, the answerphone clicked into action.

'This is Lena Peters. I'm currently unable to answer. Please leave your name and phone number after the beep and I'll call you back.'

'This is Volker Drescher. Come on, Peters, please answer – I know you're there.'

Lena picked up her passport from the dresser and put it in her pocket. *Drescher can just—!*

'I've since discovered where this idiotic idea of rifling through my desk came from,' she heard him continue.

Lena did not believe him. She walked towards the phone and was about to press the delete key, without letting Drescher finish what he had to say, when her ears suddenly pricked up.

'I know Rebecca Brandt put the idea into your head that Dr Dobelli disappeared during the investigation. Look, Peters, that's utter nonsense. I'm happy to explain. Brandt got our archivist Charlie to quietly pass her Dr Dobelli's file, which she hid in my desk.'

Lena stopped still in the hallway as though rooted to the ground, staring in disbelief at the phone.

'I've seen a text that clearly proves it. Charlie gave Brandt the file and she gave him a little cash in return. Peters, I swear to you, I had no idea what was going on. But I can tell you one thing: Brandt was jealous of you. And you fell for her little intrigue. Now don't be so damned stubborn and please pick up the phone!'

A jumble of thoughts swirled around her head as Lena took her coat from the wardrobe in the hall.

'How about you come into my office and we talk it over calmly?' Drescher suggested.

When she still did not answer the phone, he finally hung up. Lena closed her eyes for a moment to structure her thoughts. The longer she thought about it, the more what Drescher said about Brandt being jealous made sense. *Drescher thinks highly of you* – she could still hear Brandt's voice in her ears. Then she recalled how she had seen Drescher and Brandt kissing in the car park. Lena was torn. What if he turned out to be right? Brandt might have had a motive for getting her taken off the case. But could Rebecca Brandt really have pulled the wool over her eyes? Although Lena did not want to admit it, she could not deny a gnawing doubt.

But she decided not to do anything until she had spoken to Dr Dobelli and finally got some clarity. She hurried into the kitchen and put enough food out for Napoleon, in the hope that he would not devour it all in one go. Then she set off for the airport.

49

The same time, Spandau, Berlin

About half an hour after they had set off from Schöneberg, the van stopped. Gemmy heard the rear doors being opened and Artifex starting to unload the first boxes. He very carefully peeked out from under the blanket and through the open doors he saw a yard. It was deserted but for a few rubbish bins and a row of containers. As Artifex carried away two boxes, Gemmy jumped down from the load bed. He crept quietly across the yard, following Artifex into an abandoned brick house where he watched Artifex go down some stairs into the basement and disappear through a massive steel door at the bottom. He left the door slightly ajar. Gemmy followed. Although it was broad daylight outside, down here it was as dark and sombre as a tomb. The putrid stench of rotten flesh hit Gemmy as he followed Artifex through the labyrinthine basement, lurking behind at a safe distance. Artifex headed straight on to a sterile room lit by a harsh spotlight, which looked like an operating theatre. Unable to suppress his curiosity, Gemmy stood at the doorway, which had the words *Quidvis possible est – Everything is possible* – engraved above it, though Gemmy did not know enough Latin to be able to read it. He watched as Artifex pulled clamps and retractors out of a drawer. Then he slipped on a pair of rubber gloves and wiped down the operating table at the far end of the room, which had straps at the point where the arms and legs would lie. Artifex then set up the trays with scalpels, saws and drills. Gemmy's eyes widened when he noticed the congealed blood dripping from the underside of the table.

Fucking hell! That was too much blood to have come from just one person. When Artifex disappeared through the door into the next room, Gemmy, terrified, ventured a few steps into the room and looked around for somewhere he could hide. He heard Artifex coming back. Gemmy slipped behind a heavy curtain. He pulled his T-shirt over his mouth and nose and hardly dared to breathe when he caught a whiff of formaldehyde. There were several two-metre-long tanks containing a milky liquid.

What the hell? Behind them were shelves up to the ceiling, lined with various UV lamps and faceless Styrofoam heads with different wigs. Carefully, Gemmy edged over towards a narrow table, which had a book lying open on it. He picked it up and leafed through the yellowed pages. He glimpsed the anatomical sketches and handwritten notes: step-by-step instructions for amputating and preserving body parts.

Fuck, I was right – this is all way creepier than war games! Gemmy put the book back and followed the whirring of fans into the adjacent rectangular room. There was a loud buzz of blowflies and in a shaft of light he spotted an electronic device – a voice encoder, for disguising your voice. He looked up and saw a series of photos pinned to the wall. The last in the row, which looked like it was ripped out of a newspaper, was of a small, attractive woman, and there was a mobile number scrawled beneath it. Gemmy was staring closely at the picture when he heard Artifex's voice from the next room. Gemmy spun around and stood with his back against the wall beside the door. For a few seconds he stood very quietly and listened. When he realised that the voice was coming from the opposite direction, he noticed the narrow door that was half concealed behind a dusty cupboard. Gemmy crept over to it and put his ear against the door. In the background he could hear some music – an opera – and he heard Artifex's voice. It sounded like he was talking to someone.

What's he up to? Who's he talking to? He bent down to peer through the keyhole and saw Artifex talking to someone just beyond his field of vision. Gemmy tried hard not to make a sound. It was not until some time later when Artifex fell silent again and Gemmy heard the familiar sound of the van's engine from outside that he put his shoulder against the cupboard, braced himself and pushed against it with all his might, to shove it to one side. Then he opened the door to the adjacent room. It was pitch black in there and he was hit by an almost unbearable stench. Gemmy fumbled around for the light switch and turned it on. Before him he saw a room full of garish sofas, the walls lined with brightly coloured wallpaper.

Fucking hell! He had to blink and look again to make sense of what he saw – he was surrounded by old-fashioned tulle skirts, porcelain dolls and piles of sheet music. As if moving by themselves, Gemmy's legs stumbled back a few steps. Air! He needed air! His hands clasped over his mouth, as though he were gagging, he hurried back along the narrow corridor, desperate to escape.

But when he finally reached the heavy metal door, he found that it was locked.

50

The same afternoon, Edinburgh, Scotland

Exhausted after a short night and a journey that seemed like it would never end, Lena was sitting on the shuttle bus that brought passengers from Edinburgh airport into the city centre. The bus was packed and the air was stale and unpleasantly stuffy, as if the air conditioning had given up the ghost. Lena had managed to get one of the few places at a four-seater table and had stowed her bag under the seat. She took a swig from her water bottle and stared vacantly out of the window. Here and there, raindrops ran across the glass, while Lena reflected on what Belling had said about Lukas. What if the former detective chief superintendent was right and this whole trip was a waste of time? Without meaning to, she gazed at the passengers who stood crammed like sardines in the aisle. She glanced at the sullen-looking man by the door, who was nervously chewing his nails, and at the tattooed man in the baseball cap who was typing a text message on his mobile. Was that the phone Artifex had used to call her? She glanced at the blond guy in the suit, whose face was hidden behind black sunglasses but who was obviously keeping an eye on his bag. When he noticed her staring at him, she furtively turned away.

Lena Peters, for God's sake, pull yourself together! She forced herself to think of something else and rubbed her burning eyes. She had hoped to make up for her lack of sleep on the plane, but she felt so restless that she had not slept a wink. She put the water bottle to her mouth again and glanced casually at the young couple in the seats opposite her, dozing in each other's arms. The tenderness and intimacy between the two of them awakened in her a memory of Matthias. To date, he was the only man she had been able to trust, in as far as she was able to at all. He had often accused her later on of being too flippant in letting him go, and Lena had needed a while to understand why he was right. Without meaning to think about it, her thoughts drifted to their last chance encounter a little over a year ago at the University of Cologne campus. Lena had given a lecture that day on Applied Criminology, when she met Matthias in the lift. Matthias, an intelligent, friendly guy with curly hair and little dimples, had just given a presentation on his new funding programme for psychology students. Lena was very pleased to see him again, even if she rather hastily turned down his invitation to go and have a quick coffee. Matthias seemed disappointed.

'Why do you never let anyone come close to you?' he asked, as the lift doors were closing.

The question seemed pretty out of the blue to Lena. 'What do you mean? I do!' she replied, her hands buried in the pockets of her jeans and her eyes fixed on the floor indicator display on the wall of the lift.

'Oh yes?'

'Yes.'

Matthias only chuckled, and for a while there was an awkward silence between them.

'It's because of your parents, right?' he asked her. 'You're mad at them.'

Lena was horrified. 'My parents are dead, Matthias – you know that.'

But Matthias just shrugged his shoulders. 'That's why. The child in you is still angry with them for getting killed in that terrible car accident and for abandoning you and your sister. And the adult in you can no longer let anyone come close. Because then there'd be the risk you'd be abandoned again.' He just shook his head and looked down at his shoes. 'No, no – you'd rather be alone, throw yourself into your work and tell yourself that you're happy like that . . .'

Lena moved her lips to object, but she suddenly felt suffocated.

'But of course our acclaimed criminal psychologist is quite aware of that herself, is she not?' Matthias added.

At that moment, the lift doors opened on the ground floor. Matthias nodded to her briefly before he left the lift ahead of her. Speechless and with tears in her eyes, Lena followed him with her gaze.

Sitting there on the bus into Edinburgh, Lena recalled the incredible anger she had felt that day. Since then she had come to realise that Matthias was absolutely right in his assessment. And it was her own reticence and her inability to express her feelings for him that had been to blame for their relationship falling apart. Meanwhile, she had heard that Matthias was now happily married, had a thriving practice as a child psychologist in central Cologne and had a young daughter.

Dwelling on her thoughts, Lena looked out of the window again. She had squandered her chance of building a happy family. But if there was one area where her ability was uncontested, then it was her gifted skills as a criminal profiler. It was all the more important that she did not fail now and that she did everything she could to solve this case. She did not want to leave Edinburgh until Dr Dobelli had answered at least some of her questions.

51

When Lena got off the bus at Waverley Station, it was already nearly four o'clock. The station was in the heart of Edinburgh – between Old Town and New Town – and was one of the most frequented railway stations in Scotland. It was swarming with people under the old glass-domed roof and Lena had trouble finding her bearings in the hustle and bustle. Realising her phone was dead, she sighed and headed to the tourist information at the end of the large station concourse to ask for directions. When she reached the front of the queue, she passed the slip of paper with the address of Eastfield House to the chubby lady behind the counter with a pasty complexion. The woman glanced at the note, looked up and for a moment stared at Lena sceptically before typing the address into her computer. With a pronounced Scottish accent, the woman explained that the care home was just outside Edinburgh, to the east of the city. No sooner had she said this than her printer spat out the bus times and directions. Lena thanked her and went on her way.

52

The same time, Berlin

Gemmy ran and ran and did not stop. After what seemed like an eternity, lost and trapped inside Artifex's underground workshop, he had finally managed to escape through a basement window, and now all he wanted was to get as far away as possible from that unspeakable place. When he reached a small shopping street in a nearby residential area, he sank down to his knees outside an electronics shop, wiping the sweat from his forehead with the back of his hand. He would be scarred for life by what he had just seen in that cellar. He had underestimated Artifex and could not deny that in some ways he was quite impressed by the ghastly scene. Nevertheless, he promised himself never to step foot in that basement again and to keep a distance from Artifex for the time being. Lost in thought, Gemmy stared up at the large flat-screen television in the window, which was showing the trailer of the new Hollywood action movie starring Jeffrey Maloney.

'More action, more horror, more goose bumps . . .' he heard through the small outdoor speakers above the shop window.

Gemmy shook his head. He was just about to get up and go when his attention was caught by a news item about a series of unsolved murders. Gemmy stopped dead in front of the shop window.

'The number of cruelly mutilated murder victims has since grown rapidly, while the police are still fumbling about in the dark.'

When the picture of a certain Carmen Martinez appeared, and at the same time the news reporter spoke of an amputated nose, Gemmy held his breath. The freezer bag in Artifex's icebox!

With a mounting sense of anxiety, he continued to stare at the TV. Footage appeared from a press conference last week. Then the camera shifted from the reporter over to a slightly short man who was introduced as head of the homicide division and who hurried past the journalists into the police headquarters without making a comment. Gemmy's face froze when in the background behind the head of Homicide he saw a young woman who he immediately recognised as the one in the photo in Artifex's cellar. Without a doubt, it was the same person. A shiver went down Gemmy's spine. But a moment later the corners of his mouth rose into a smile. Gemmy had never considered himself to be particularly bright, but at the sight of this woman he had a fiendish idea.

53

Late afternoon, Edinburgh

After a long bus journey and a good fifteen-minute walk through some woodland, Lena eventually reached the gates of Eastfield House. The sky was overcast, suggesting a storm was brewing, as Lena approached the porter's lodge.

'Hello, my name's Peters. I'm here to see a patient – Dr Dobelli,' she said in English, in a friendly tone.

The porter – an elderly man with a puffy face – looked as though he had long been part of the furniture. He eyed her for a moment, frowning. His eyes were a dark, greyish blue, like the sky over Edinburgh.

'You know that visiting hours are nearly over?'

Lena nodded and gave the doorman a polite smile. She was tired. She could come back the next day, by appointment, she explained, but she did not want to lose any time and after the long journey she had had it would be a shame not to get to speak to Dr Dobelli, at least briefly. She saw how the man's wrinkly hands trembled as he noted down her name and the precise time of her arrival, to the minute. A quick peek at the list told Lena that she was the only visitor to the home that day – that week, in fact.

'Miss, your bag, please.' The old man rose from his chair, pointing his pen at Lena's overnight bag. 'I'll have to ask you to leave your bag here. Those are the rules.'

He stepped out of the side door. Lena reluctantly handed it over to him. Shortly afterwards, he opened the gates into the grounds. From the corner of her eye, Lena saw the old man stare after her with a stern expression and then pick up the telephone as she headed along the gravel path up to the Victorian manor house.

In front of it stood a number of oak trees, hundreds of years old, whose treetops loomed far above the massive columns and the mansard roof. At least outwardly, the building looked more like an old castle to Lena than a care home. Only the bars on the windows were a reminder that here, behind closed doors, mentally ill patients were being treated. Lena had visited many psychiatric institutions, and she found them strangely fascinating, as though their walls harboured an ancient secret.

She was met on the stairs up to the front door by an ageless, fierce-looking nurse with a stack of files under her arm. Lena was aware that she had not reached her destination yet and her conversation with Dobelli possibly depended on getting past this matron.

Good afternoon, I'm Lena Peters. I'm a criminal psychologist and I would like to ask Dr Cornelia Dobelli some questions about a series of murders. Lena formulated her introduction to herself. *Too direct!*

'Good afternoon, I'm Lena Peters. I'm an old friend of Dr Dobelli,' she said finally, holding out her hand.

The sister showed no sign of offering her hand to shake, but inspected Lena. 'Do you have an appointment?'

Lena dropped her outstretched hand and gave a polite smile. 'No, but—'

'Then I'm sorry. Visitors are only received by appointment.'

'Listen, I've come all the way from Berlin especially to see Cornelia Dobelli. It's about an urgent private matter – an inheritance.' Lena was amazed at the words that came pouring out. 'It is very important.' And that was not a lie.

The nurse gave her a quizzical look. 'Wait here,' she said. She left Lena standing on the steps and disappeared through the front door into the building.

Lena waited with her arms crossed, standing with her back to the door, and gazed over at the barbed wire fence that surrounded the grounds of the care home. A moment later, she heard a deep voice from behind her.

'You wanted to see Dr Dobelli?'

Lena turned around to see a clean-shaven middle-aged man in a dark suit and freshly shined leather shoes. He introduced himself as Ronald Smith, director of the care home. Lena wondered whether all visitors were personally received by the director or whether this was just for Dr Dobelli.

'That's right,' she said, standing up straight.

The man ran a hand through his greying hair. 'You said you were a friend?'

'Yes.'

He nodded. 'All right, if you'd follow me, please.' Mr Smith walked ahead down the stairs.

'Dr Dobelli is in Woodford House,' he explained, as Lena followed him along the gravel path around the building. They walked past the staff quarters and up to a large brick building, not far from a small lake in the woods.

Once they were inside Woodford House, Mr Smith led her through a power-assisted glass door and along a corridor, where she could smell dinner and mint tea. At the end of the corridor an elderly lady approached them, babbling something under her breath, which Lena could not make out. Lena looked away and followed Mr Smith into the magnolia lounge furnished by little more than a few chairs, two tables and a television.

At the far end of the room, by the window overlooking the grounds, sat a dark-haired woman in a grey cardigan. She had her back turned to them and was reading a book.

Ronald Smith cleared his throat. 'Dr Dobelli, you have a visitor.'

The woman made no attempt to turn and face them. Lena gave her a moment. She pushed her hands into her pockets and looked around a moment longer. Besides Dr Dobelli, in the lounge there was a hunched little man walking around a table with a game of chess laid out on it, his index finger held intently to his lower lip. The man's eyes were different colours and he grinned at Lena as he scratched at the blotchy, flaky skin on his face. *Symptoms of a severe psychosomatic disease,* thought Lena, before turning her attention back to Dr Dobelli. When Lena walked towards her, it struck her immediately that she was holding the book upside down. Dr Dobelli herself seemed not to have noticed this.

'Dr Dobelli?' Lena tried again.

No response.

She nodded politely to Ronald Smith, to indicate that she would like to speak to her alone. After a moment's hesitation, he agreed and walked away. Lena was standing behind Dr Dobelli, to one side.

'Hello, I'm Lena Peters. I've come from Berlin,' she began cautiously, speaking in German. 'I'm . . .' She lowered her eyes furtively. 'I was your successor in the homicide team, if you like,' she said outright, assuming that the other patient would not understand her. 'I was withdrawn from the case before I had really begun,' Lena confessed.

Very slowly, the woman turned to look at her. From her research Lena knew that Dr Cornelia Dobelli was forty-two. But the woman who sat before her looked much older, with her gaunt, weary-looking face. There was a stripe of grey hair at the roots of her thin black hair, which fell over her bony shoulders.

'So he still hasn't been caught . . .' she said in a whisper, looking at Lena with a nervous twitch in her left eye. 'Trust me – being withdrawn from the case is the best thing that could have happened to you.' Dr Dobelli studied her closely. 'How did you find me?'

Lena chewed on her lower lip, wondering what to say. Eventually she decided to try telling the truth.

Dr Dobelli probed her with her eyes. 'Who knows that I'm here except for you and this Lukas?'

'Nobody.'

The woman looked frightened. 'You're sure?'

Lena nodded reassuringly and noticed the scars on the insides of Dr Dobelli's forearms, which stretched from the cuffs of her cardigan to the wrists. They were cuts such as Lena had seen most often in people who had slashed themselves with a razor, a knife or broken glass to relieve their emotional pain.

'Shall we play chess?!' cried the red-faced man, interrupting the brief moment of silence. The invitation prompted the corners of Lena's mouth to turn up into a friendly smile.

'I'm afraid you'll have to find another opponent.'

But the man persisted. He jumped like a rubber ball from one leg to the other and scratched his cheeks with both hands. 'Just one game! If you beat me, I'll tell you everything I know!'

Her ears pricking up, Lena asked Dr Dobelli, 'What does he mean by that?'

'Ignore him,' groaned Dr Dobelli. 'Numpy's a bore, that's all – isn't that right, Numpy?'

He grinned. 'I know something you don't know . . .' he hissed at Lena.

Dr Dobelli stood up. After a fleeting glance over her shoulder, she said, 'Come on, let's have a little walk in the grounds, and we can talk without any interruptions.'

54

The extensive formal garden, with its fountains and ornamental clipped hedges, seemed well tended and Lena wondered whether the patients who walked around here day after day were as well cared for. At the far end, the grounds bordered onto a fenced-off lake, to which presumably only certain patients had access. Dr Dobelli seemed to belong to that group of patients, because she headed straight towards it.

'So you're still pursuing the case unofficially, I gather,' she returned to the topic once they had passed the gate through to the lake, and Lena registered the suspicious glances of some passing nurses. 'If, however, you've come to hear my assessment of the offender profile, I'm afraid I'll have to disappoint you. I want nothing more to do with the case!'

Lena bit her lip. What she heard was the voice of a deeply frightened woman, which presumably had nothing in common with the person Dr Dobelli must once have been. It was not enough to satisfy Lena, however.

'Dr Dobelli, nobody else is as familiar with the offender's character traits as you,' said Lena, walking at her side as they approached a narrow jetty. 'Who or what has made you so afraid that you do not want to talk about the case?'

'Like I said, I'm afraid you could have saved yourself the trouble of coming all the way to Edinburgh.'

Lena was not about to give up as quickly as that. Dr Dobelli started to pick up her pace, as if she wanted to run away from Lena's questions.

'Please wait!' Lena overtook her on the jetty and stood in her way. 'The killer called me the other night,' she finally blurted out.

Dr Dobelli stopped, thunderstruck. Lena looked her straight in the eye, but Dobelli's expression was unfathomable. Suddenly something changed in her expression, and the nervous twitch in her eye returned. Dr Dobelli seemed to pluck up the courage to speak, then her face went deathly pale. She staggered and sank to her knees.

Oh my God! 'Dr Dobelli – are you OK?' cried Lena, alarmed. She took Dr Dobelli's arm and tried to help her up.

The woman groaned. 'It's fine . . . Let me be. I just need to sit down a moment, that's all.'

'Should I call a nurse?'

'No, no . . . no need.' She sat awkwardly on the edge of the jetty, leaning her weight on her hands. Her feet dangled over the water. When Lena saw that her complexion had returned to normal, she sat down beside her and was just about to say something when her mobile rang. Lena reached into the pocket of her trench coat and looked at the screen. It was Wulf Belling. The timing could hardly have been worse, but Belling would hardly call her in Edinburgh if it was not genuinely important.

Lena glanced at Cornelia Dobelli. 'I'm sorry, I'll be right back,' she said and got up quickly.

'Yes? What's wrong?' she said in a low voice, walking a few steps along the jetty with the phone to her ear. 'Of course I'm still in Edinburgh, and it's not great timing.'

'Your sister is an absolute nightmare to live with!' came Belling's voice down the line. He sounded pretty outraged.

Lena closed her eyes briefly and suppressed a sigh. 'I know. I told you – Tamara isn't easy to get on with.'

'Not easy?' Belling exclaimed. 'Tamara is a complete disaster! Our phone bill has gone through the roof thanks to her, she's nearly burned the house down because she's so clumsy, she sits in front of the TV the whole day, and to top it all she leaves her stuff lying around everywhere, including the baby's shitty nappies!' She heard him wheeze. 'And now she's even started smoking spliffs! With the baby in her arms! In the middle of my living room! As if we haven't had enough of that with my own daughter. You would not believe what a struggle it was to get Marietta off that stuff!'

Lena chewed on the inside of her cheek and lowered her eyes. She was ashamed of her twin sister's behaviour and it made her infinitely sad that, time and time again, Tamara managed to push away the people who were trying to help her.

'Listen, I'm so sorry about all of this . . . But let's talk about it when I get back, OK?'

With that, she ended the call, immediately annoyed with herself at having answered it in the first place. Lena went back over to Dr Dobelli and sat down beside her on the jetty. While she was still trying to work out how best to pick up the thread again, Dr Dobelli surprised her by speaking first.

'I should never have accepted the case,' she said, her eyes still fixed on the lake. The ice was broken. Lena raised her eyebrows, intrigued to know what was coming next.

'There's a man,' Dr Dobelli began, speaking in a more conciliatory tone now. 'I was quite close to him, if you understand what I mean . . . He runs a modern art gallery in Berlin. At least that's what it looks like from the outside. In fact, he sells preserved human body parts to wealthy customers around the world. He's had outrageous sums for them from Japan and the US,' she said and shook her head. 'I dread to think how sick the artist must be who's behind those perverted creations.'

Lena jumped up. 'But of course! In the phone call he described himself as an artist – it could very well be the same man. Volker Drescher and his team have considered all kinds of possibilities but so far they haven't thought of that.' She sensed that she was on the right track. She had to ask, 'Why did you not say something earlier?'

Dr Cornelia Dobelli looked up, her eyes glazed over. 'I was afraid.'

'Of what?'

'This man, my ex . . .' She pulled her cardigan tightly around her. 'It's because of him that I'm here.' She was clearly struggling to talk about it. And as soon as she had uttered the words, the nervous twitch in her eye came back.

Lena gave her a compassionate look and asked, 'What's the name of this artist?'

'I don't know.'

Lena studied her profile, determined not to give up.

'Did he ever mention the name Artifex?'

Cornelia Dobelli looked like she was thinking. Then she shook her head. 'One day, when I made the mistake of asking him about this artist, he totally freaked out . . . He beat me black and blue and made my life hell ever since.' She looked up briefly and then lowered her gaze again. 'He started stalking me and for weeks I'd see him following me. Day and night he'd be there watching me, wherever I least expected him, to the extent that sometimes I'd see him when he wasn't even there . . .' She looked anxiously at Lena. 'This man . . . you'd know him by his tattoo . . .' She pointed to her neck as if to show where it was. 'He's . . . he's dangerous. If he finds out where I am, he will kill me.'

Lena could literally feel this woman's fear. 'What is his name?' she asked.

But the response she hoped for never came. Lena's heartbeat began to race, pounding faster the longer that Dr Dobelli's silence pressed down on her.

'Dr Dobelli, you must tell me what his name is!'

55

'Dr Dobelli, if the murders in Berlin are to come to an end, then you need to tell me—' She broke off when she saw the stern-looking nurse hurrying along the jetty towards them with two uniformed security guards in tow.

'Visiting hours are over. Kindly leave the grounds immediately,' she instructed Lena.

Feeling harassed, Lena looked at Dr Dobelli and then again at the nurse. 'Could you give us just a minute longer, please,' Lena asked, holding up her index finger.

'I'm sorry, but that's the protocol.' The nurse nodded to the two men for them to accompany Lena to the exit.

'Thank you, I know the way,' Lena said quietly, getting up to go. As she walked away, she turned back again to Dr Dobelli. 'What's his name?' she called out to her, as the two security guards urged her along the jetty back to the bank. But Dr Dobelli just watched her silently.

'Shit!' Lena said under her breath, cursing the fact that her visit had been a complete waste of time and doubting her instincts, when suddenly Cornelia Dobelli called back, 'Semak! His name's Oleg Semak – the same name as the gallery!'

Although the two bulky security guards had still not let go of her, Lena felt in an instant like a ton of weight had fallen off her shoulders.

'Thank you,' she said, although Dr Dobelli was already out of earshot.

56

Wulf Belling sat under cover of darkness behind the wheel of his Peugeot, a cigarette dangling from his mouth as he watched Ferdinand Roggendorf through his binoculars. The lanky young man was dressed in black and was gesturing wildly while speaking on his mobile, as he paced through his brightly lit apartment in a new building on the other side of the street. Although only Roggendorf knew what it was he was so upset about, Belling couldn't help feeling a twinge of schadenfreude. But before he knew it, Roggendorf had disappeared from the window.

Without really knowing what he was hoping to achieve, Belling decided to keep an eye on the house for a while longer. He flicked the ash from his cigarette out of the window, and in the same second his mobile started ringing. He put the binoculars down on the passenger seat and answered the phone. It was his daughter and, much to his surprise, her tone was even quite friendly.

'Listen, Jetta,' Belling began, immediately filled with regret. 'That's fine, Marietta. As for the drugs—' He stopped short and snorted. 'Well of course marijuana's a drug! . . . What? . . .

OK, we'll leave it for now, but I could hardly tell from the smell that it was left over from last time, and . . . What? No, of course, but . . .' He listened to Marietta and closed his weary eyes before he abruptly tore them open a moment later. 'You want what?! . . . Two thousand euros?!' He gave a feeble laugh. 'What gave you that idea? I mean, where am I supposed to get that kind of money from out of the blue?' His voice cracked. 'And what do you need it for anyway?' Tense, he drew on his cigarette and shook his head. 'No, of course I trust you – but as your father I'd say I've got the right to know why you need so much money so desperately!' Fearing his daughter would see him as a complete failure, he and Helena had decided not to tell Marietta for the time being that he was out of a job. Yet again it occurred to him that it was probably time to be straight with his daughter. But just like every other time he had wanted to, he couldn't quite summon up the courage.

'France? Aha, and I'm supposed to just believe that?' A longer pause this time. 'No, I didn't mean it like that – I do believe you, but—' Suddenly he saw Ferdinand Roggendorf leave the apartment block with two burly men, their faces shaded by black baseball caps. And as Marietta carried on cursing him at the other end of the line, Belling watched as they walked towards a dark-coloured van on the other side of the street. If he was not mistaken, Ferdinand Roggendorf was carrying the same sports bag that he had with him the other day at the old gasworks. With his mobile phone pressed against his ear, Belling slumped down in his seat, hoping not to be seen, when suddenly he dropped his cigarette.

'Ow, shit!' Awkwardly he bent down to reach for the burning cigarette. 'What? . . . Uh, no, of course I'm listening,' he assured his daughter, while he frantically and clumsily fumbled around with one hand in the footwell. When he finally found the cigarette and sat up again at the wheel, his daughter had already hung up.

And Ferdinand Roggendorf, together with his retinue, had vanished into thin air.

'Damn it!' exclaimed Belling and slapped his hand furiously against the steering wheel.

57

It was almost midnight when Lena stopped in at Biddy Mulli-
gans, a crowded Irish pub in the lively Grassmarket in the heart of
the Old Town and just a few minutes' walk from the guesthouse
where Lena had booked a room for the night. Inside the pub it
was noisy and rammed full. A three-piece band were belting out
a mix of folk and jazz, while a few revellers squeezed onto a tiny
dance floor, jostled by drinkers on all sides. Lena sat down at the
bar and ordered a drink from the barman, who introduced himself as Eddy. She took out her black notebook and flipped through
her notes, deep in thought. It was barely a minute before Eddy
presented her with her pint and launched into a verbose story
about how the likes of Gerry Rafferty, who long after his death
was still renowned far beyond the borders of Scotland for his song
'Baker Street' and who was known to grace this pub for a drink
or two. Lena nodded and tried to smile. He clearly knew from her
accent that she wasn't a local. At another point in her life, were she
here in Edinburgh as a tourist, she would not have been averse to
a little digression about the city and its residents, but right now all
she could think about was her visit to see Dr Cornelia Dobelli at
the care home. She put her glass to her lips and recalled what Dr
Dobelli said about Oleg Semak. She took a swig of beer and put
her glass down. She had noted his name in her notebook and now

she was circling her pen around it, distracted, when her mobile beeped. It was a text. Lena glanced at the screen and smiled when she saw that it was from Lukas.

How's it going in Scotland?

Smiling, Lena typed: **I think I'm making progress. Thank you for your help.** She sent the message and put her phone away again.

When she got back to Berlin she would do something for Lukas to repay the favour. But first she would go over to this gallery and check it out.

Lena decided she'd have this one beer then call it a night. She had a lot to do tomorrow and would need to be at her best.

58

Meanwhile in Friedenau, Berlin

'I don't believe it!' Wulf Belling was appalled to get home late at night and find Tamara yet again sitting in front of the TV with a joint in her hand. And yet again the place looked as if a bomb had hit. 'I told you – I will not have this damned stuff in my house!'

'Oh, you old killjoy,' teased Tamara, who had made herself comfortable on the sofa with a pizza. That very moment, Marcel – who was lying on a blanket beside her on the couch – started crying.

Belling grabbed the joint from the young woman's hand and rammed it into her can of Coke.

'Hey, man, that cost a bomb!' Tamara took her crossed legs off the coffee table and pushed up the strap of the negligée she was wearing, which she had pilfered from Helena's wardrobe.

Belling looked pitifully at the baby. 'Have you any idea how much harm you're doing to the child with that shitty stuff?' Waving his hand about, he went over to the window to let in some fresh air. 'You really are worse than my daughter – except that Marietta's at a difficult age, whereas you're just a lost cause!' he snapped. 'It's bad enough to let your own life go to the dogs, but you damn well need to pull yourself together and not screw up your son's life while you're at it!' With a grunt, he picked up the crisp packets that were lying around. 'My God, you really are good for nothing!' The second he uttered those words he regretted it. But it was too late. Tamara suddenly burst into tears. She picked up the baby and stood up, sobbing, her tears dripping onto Marcel's little face. Belling looked at her with his lips squeezed together. 'I'm sorry, I didn't mean it.'

'It's OK. Marcel and I won't burden you any longer.' She picked the baby's blanket up off the sofa and walked with the child in her arms over to the door.

'No, wait a second!' Helplessly, he lifted up his arms. He pulled her head to his shoulder and gave her and the baby a comforting hug, and at that very moment the door to the living room was pushed open and in came Marietta, who hadn't shown her face all day.

'What the hell's going on here?!' she asked in horror, as her eyes, black with eyeliner, narrowed to thin slits. Belling let go of Tamara, but before he could say anything Marietta had already stormed out into the hallway. Belling rushed out after his daughter.

'Marietta! Wait! It's not what you think!'

Marietta grabbed her backpack from the wardrobe in the hall and shook her head angrily. 'Oh yeah? And what's this woman doing here in our house wearing mum's things?!'

'That . . . that I can't explain right now.'

'What's this supposed to be? Revenge for the surgeon Mum's run off with?' She snorted. 'Could you not at least find a woman who's even vaguely close to your age?!'

Belling gasped. 'Jetta, please – that is really going too far!'

'How many times have I told you – don't call me Jetta!' she snapped. She was almost out of the front door when she exclaimed, 'What is it then – is she earning her keep? Is that why we're skint?! And what's with the baby? It wouldn't surprise me if it was yours!'

'You do not talk to your father like that!'

'I hate you! Mum was right to walk out!' Marietta screamed and than ran out into the night.

Belling could feel his blood pounding in his head. 'Damn it, Jetta! Where do you think you're going so late at night?' he shouted out into the front garden.

'None of your business!' she yelled and ran onto the pavement.

'Oh yes it is, young lady! As long as you are living under my roof and you're not yet eighteen, it damn well is my business!'

But she was already out of earshot. Belling tore at his hair and ran after her, panting. *This cannot be happening!*

He didn't want to believe his eyes when he saw Marietta stop at the next street corner and disappear into a black Mercedes. Beside himself with worry, he sprinted back to his car and drove off in pursuit.

59

That same night, Edinburgh

It had got considerably cooler and Lena did up her coat as she walked, shivering, along the cobbled street, past the historic buildings in Edinburgh's medieval old town. A cold wind brushed by her and billowed the fabric of her trench coat, while Lena tried to unfold her map to check she was on the right road to her guesthouse. According to the description on the website that she had booked the room through, it seemed like it shouldn't be much further. As she turned the corner, she almost bumped into a man in a kilt, who was standing stock-still like a statue under a street lamp. Lena apologised, threw a few coins into his pot and walked on quickly. Further ahead was a group of tourists bellowing at the top of their voices and dressed as though they had come straight from the Fringe Festival. As they turned off towards Edinburgh Castle, which was impressively lit up at night, Lena carried on towards the guesthouse along one of the countless winding streets. She briefly thought of all the legends and ghost stories she'd heard about Edinburgh's dark alleyways, but the next minute she laughed at herself. She walked on a few more steps, then turned into the next lane. No sooner had she shaken off the idea, when she suddenly heard footsteps behind her.

Lena stopped and looked around. In the alley everything was quiet. But there it was once again: the vague feeling she was being followed, the feeling that had clung to her like a shadow since the phone call from the killer, and that she had only momentarily chased away during her brief visit to see Dr Dobelli.

Was he here in Edinburgh? Had he followed her from the pub? She picked up her pace and started to run across the cobble stones.

Well, if someone's been following, they seem to have vanished into thin air, she thought, as she saw the lit-up name of the guesthouse at the end of the alleyway. Lena was just about to run the last stretch when, all of a sudden, a dark figure sprang out from a side alley and blocked her path. She froze, her fists clenched ready to defend herself, as a man with his face obscured by his hood suddenly turned and dashed towards her. He was aiming for her bag. All her belongings were in it, so Lena had no intention of letting it go without putting up a fight. The man tugged at her bag and a violent scuffle ensued. But her attacker was physically stronger than Lena and had the element of surprise. He knocked her back with a strong blow to the stomach. Lena saw white dots before her eyes, and as she bent over in pain, gasping for breath, she saw the man run away with her bag.

60

Late at night, Friedrichshain, Berlin

Wulf Belling was sitting behind the wheel of his car, watching as Marietta got out of the Mercedes with two shady figures, who were definitely not her classmates – they looked much older.

I'm sure I've come across you guys before back in Narcotics.

The three walked through the grounds of the former Ostbahnhof station to a large concrete building where there seemed to be a nightclub. They walked right past the long queue of people ready to party and, after a brief handshake with the bouncer, disappeared into the club.

If you come near my daughter with any kind of substance, I will annihilate you with my own hands!

Belling turned off the engine and decided to go and keep an eye on his daughter. He got out and also walked right up to the front of the queue, heading purposefully for the entrance where a hefty bald-headed bouncer blocked his path with his arms folded.

'Hey, Grandpa, aintcha a bit old?'

'You need to let me in!'

The man in the bomber jacket laughed. 'You're probably not the only one who thinks that.' He waved his hand, gesturing at the queue.

'I'm not here to have fun.' With a determined expression, he held up his police ID.

'Why didn't you say so?' With a fake, overly friendly smile, the doorman stepped aside and let him pass.

The old trick – good to see it still works, thought Belling as he entered the heaving nightclub. As he looked around, he rapidly lost all hope of ever finding Marietta here. It was dark, and all around him danced strange creatures that moved like robots under the strobe lighting. And then this deafening, pounding music. It was not as if he had never been to the odd nightclub in his time, but Berlin's techno culture was completely alien to him.

Besides, it was so overwhelmingly cramped and hot that he felt his lungs were being starved of oxygen. He fought his way on through the crowds, until he finally spotted Marietta with her dubious companions. Belling squinted to see her clearly. He could not believe his eyes when, at that precise moment, he saw one of the two men slipping her a pill. Time stood still for a second before Belling stormed through the mass of ravers without pausing to think. Marietta was just about to drop the pill into her mouth when he dived in front of her out of nowhere and knocked the tablet right out of her hand, sending it flying into the crowd.

'Dad!' Marietta grimaced and stared at him with her mouth hanging open, as if she had seen a ghost. 'For God's sake! What are you doing here?'

'I might ask you the same question!' he shouted against the music. 'You gave me a solemn promise that you would keep off the drugs!'

'I am!'

'She's right, man!' One of the two guys stepped forwards and held out a packet to prove it to him. Belling looked at the package:

Aspirin. For a moment, the pounding roar retreated into the background and Belling heard nothing but the blood rushing through his head. Then he looked at the faces of Marietta's companions, who admittedly looked much younger than he had thought and perhaps not quite so threatening. Wulf Belling longed for the ground to open and swallow him up. His cheeks burned red as he looked at his daughter and yet again felt like a complete failure.

'My God, Dad, you're so embarrassing!' Marietta snapped, throwing him a hateful look and then turning her back to him. And as she disappeared in a huff into the crowd, the two young men shrugged him off with a pitying shake of the head.

'Just watch it – I'm a cop and I can bring you in for the night, you know!' Belling threatened. Now he really felt stupid. It was desperation that had spoken. And it was high time to go.

Annoyed and embarrassed, Belling made his way back through the club to the exit. Once outside, he took some deep breaths. The bass still boomed in his ears as he hurriedly lit a cigarette and walked over to his car. He hadn't gone far when, in the car park, he spotted a familiar face. Belling stopped in his tracks.

Well, look here – if it isn't our lawyer's son!

Ferdinand Roggendorf was alone and must have left the club just before him.

Just you wait, you're not going to get away from me this time, he thought to himself as he watched Roggendorf on the other side of the car park getting into his black van.

Belling hurried over to his Peugeot as Roggendorf started the engine. He reached his car to find – to his dismay – that another driver had blocked him in. Roggendorf was already pulling out of his parking space. Belling could do nothing but watch idly as Roggendorf yet again evaded capture.

61

Sunday afternoon, 15th May

When Lena walked into Bacon 'n' Cheese at just after half past twelve, Wulf Belling was already sitting at the counter, half hidden behind his newspaper. Lena hadn't been able to get through to him again after her visit to Dr Dobelli, but fortunately she had texted him – before she was mugged – to suggest they meet at noon at Bacon 'n' Cheese. The cafe was much busier than usual and Belling didn't notice Lena come in. She was more than twenty minutes late and desperately hoped he would still be waiting. But Belling seemed so engrossed in the day's headlines that he did not seem to have noticed. He looked rough – he had bags under his eyes and a five o'clock shadow. And even though it wasn't long after midday, she saw from the glass the waitress cleared away as she hurried past that he wasn't just having coffee. No sooner had Lena sat down on the free bar stool beside him than Belling lowered the paper and looked up.

'Have you heard? Our friend has struck again.' He put the newspaper down on the counter and pointed at the headline.

Lena nodded. 'I saw on the flight back.' The fact that she had been unable to prevent another gruesome murder troubled her far more than she wanted to let on. The image of every murder victim was burned irrevocably into her memory and, in her eyes, each one reflected her own failure.

'All that's been announced officially is that it was a British tourist, middle-aged, found early this morning in Monbijou Park with her breasts cut off.' Shaking his head, he grimaced. 'Her breasts – Jesus Christ!'

Lena looked down at the paper and felt her chest tightening at the thought of it.

'I hope you've brought better news back from Scotland. I've been trying to ring you all morning,' he said, looking at her expectantly.

'Well, you could have been trying for a long time,' she replied, and told him about the attack the night before. 'I was just lucky that my passport and return ticket were in my pocket, not the bag, or else I would have lost them too.'

Belling sighed and shook his head. 'Did you go to the police?'

'Of course, but what difference does it make? I was told the same as every other tourist the whole world over: "If your bag shows up, we'll let you know."' She shook her head. 'I'm still fuming. I've lost not just my mobile and a thousand other things, but also my notebook.'

Belling's ears pricked up. 'Your notebook?' He looked at her inquisitively. 'Any chance it wasn't a coincidence that your bag was stolen?'

When Lena realised what he was getting at, she shook her head. 'I think it's unlikely,' she said, looking up to catch the waitress's eyes.

'Don't tell me that's all you have to report from Edinburgh?'

Lena smiled. 'Not at all.' She told him about her conversation with Dr Dobelli. And about the owner of the gallery.

'Well, if that's so, we should pay this Oleg Semak a little visit,' said Belling, when Lena had finished her story.

She grinned. 'Already been.'

His face showed a look of disbelief. 'You went round there on your own, without letting me know?'

'How could I, without a mobile phone? And that's where I'd saved your number.'

'Hmm, true.'

'I didn't want to waste time. So I went there straight from the airport,' she said, and quickly ordered an espresso from the waitress as she dashed past; Lena recognised her from last time. 'The gallery is near Kottbusser Tor. It looks pretty run down from the outside. You wouldn't just pop in unless you were explicitly looking for it.'

Belling stared at her. 'And? Did you manage to suss out this Semak guy?'

She shook her head. 'I didn't even go inside.'

'Why not? You went all the way to the gallery but didn't go inside?'

Lena squinted. 'I was just walking towards it when at that precise moment I saw Volker Drescher heading in.'

'What are you saying?' Belling leaned in towards her.

'As you can imagine, I was as surprised as you. Anyway, I thought it wise to come back another time.'

'Indeed,' commented Belling and took a moment to reflect on her words. There was a short silence. 'It's all rather strange . . .' Belling muttered after a while.

Lena nodded. 'Somewhat.'

Then Wulf Belling uttered the question that had been hang-ing unspoken in the air between them. 'What if Drescher is somehow involved in this?'

Lena chewed thoughtfully on her fingernail. Then she shook her head. 'I don't know . . . Maybe he's just further along in the case than we are and he's also just keeping an eye on the place?'

Belling looked at Lena for a moment, thinking. He had never made a secret of the fact that he could not stand Volker Drescher. But after considering it for a while, the idea did seem absurd. 'You're probably right. That puffed-up short-arse doesn't have the balls to pull something like this off,' he said contemptuously. 'But this Semak . . . we should pay him a visit ASAP. Whatever Drescher was doing at the gallery – it won't take all day.'

Lena glanced at her watch. 'Let's give him a little longer.'

'Whatever you say,' he muttered, as the waitress brought over Lena's espresso.

'What about Suzanna Wirt's work colleagues?' she asked. 'Anything to report?'

'Nope,' he answered, shaking his head. 'I talked to just about every employee at Cenrat Media who might have plausibly worked with her. Apparently, although Suzanna was popular and everyone liked her, nobody was particularly close friends with her. Anyway, none of her colleagues could tell me what she got up to at the weekend or with whom.'

Lena sipped her coffee and looked at him questioningly over the rim of her cup. 'Any other news?'

Belling played with a beer mat, as though it took him some effort to utter the following words. 'Ferdinand Roggendorf . . . He's not our man,' he managed to say through gritted teeth.

Confused, Lena wrinkled her forehead. 'And what makes you so sure?'

'Because I know from a reliable source that the tourist in Monbijou Park died immediately after the amputation. Which was last night, shortly after one a.m., when Roggendorf has an alibi.'

'Aha. And his alibi is watertight?'

'I *am* his alibi,' he added, reluctantly.

Lena could not quite follow him.

'I saw him at the time in question coming out of a techno club in Friedrichshain,' Belling added by way of an explanation. 'So he can't have killed the tourist. Since there seems to be no doubt that it was the work of the infamous Mutilator, like it or not, Roggendorf can be excluded from the circle of suspects.'

This made sense to Lena. While Belling was struggling with his disappointment, Lena felt her assessment was confirmed: that Ferdinand Roggendorf and Artifex were not one and the same person. She had not excluded the possibility that he was in some way connected with the murders, but for her there had never been any doubt that he was not the perpetrator. Roggendorf simply did not fit the profile. No, these murders were not Roggendorf's style. And if she was completely honest with herself, she was relieved that her instincts had not let her down. But there was one question Lena could not resist asking.

'And what were you doing in a techno club?' She tried to suppress an amused smile.

Belling, who was usually up for a laugh, showed no change in expression. 'To cut a long story short: I had a spot of bother with

Marietta again. A misunderstanding . . . to do with your sister,' he said with a dismissive hand gesture.

'With Tamara? Oh no, what's she done now?' She phrased it as a question, but in fact she did not really want to hear the answer.

'What can I say . . . I found her with a joint again,' he reported, shaking his head. 'This time I really gave her a piece of my mind. I flew off the handle . . . and . . . well, maybe I was a bit harsh,' he confessed, pulling at his earlobe. 'Suddenly she burst into tears. I felt terrible. So I went over and gave her a hug.' He raised his arms as if to act out the gesture. 'And just then who should walk in but Marietta. She must have taken it in the wrong way, because she completely freaked out . . . She ran out of the house, and I ran out after her.'

Lena studied his face. 'And then?'

'Then I followed her to this techno joint, because I thought . . .' He pressed his lips together and shook his head. 'Oh, it doesn't matter. Anyway, it was when I left the nightclub that I saw Roggendorf.'

'And you're sure that it was him?'

'It was definitely Ferdinand Roggendorf – as sure as eggs is eggs.'

Lena finished her coffee and put the cup down. 'And where's Tamara now?'

'I don't know.' He raised his hands in a clueless gesture, then placed them on the counter. 'When I got back late last night, Tamara and the baby had gone.'

Lena frowned. 'Do you have any idea where she might have gone?' she asked, concerned.

Belling shook his head. 'I assume they'll come back at some point today . . . After all, she's left her bags at ours.'

'Her bags?' This worried Lena. Tamara never had much, but whatever belongings she had she always kept with her. Lena hoped to God that Tamara hadn't done anything foolish.

'May I?' she asked, pointing to Belling's mobile, which was lying on the counter.

'Sure, I've got your sister's number saved, just in case.'

Lena nodded and dialled Tamara's number. 'It's switched off,' she said after a while, handing the phone back to him.

Belling scratched his forehead. 'She seems a bit challenging, your sister.' He looked questioningly at Lena. 'Why did you actually do all of this for her?'

'What do you mean?' Lena asked. She ordered another espresso.

'Well, everything, I mean. You take care of your sister although she only thinks about herself and doesn't care in the slightest how other people feel.'

Lena shrugged. 'Well, she's still my sister. You have to take people as they are . . .' she said, more to herself than to him, and for an absentminded moment she turned the sugar dispenser around in her hand. 'When Tamara and I went to live with different foster families after our parents died, a few years went by when we didn't see each other.' She stared at the sugar dispenser as she talked. 'That changed when we reached eighteen. For a while we were inseparable. But then Tamara got together with the wrong guy and somehow we lost contact again.' The waitress brought Lena her espresso. She took a deep breath before she continued. 'With time, Tamara's husband turned out to be more and more of a tyrant – he was very violent and he would regularly beat the living day-lights out of her.' Without raising her head, Lena looked up at Belling. 'You have no idea how many times I took her in and I did everything I could to persuade her to leave him once and for all. But she always went back to him.' Lena shook her head sadly. 'It was only after the birth of her daughter Fabienne that Tamara's eyes were opened finally. She never admitted it, but I think he also used to take his anger out on the little girl.' Lena tucked a strand of hair behind her ear before she continued, deep in thought. 'I still remember the day when she drove home for the last time to pack her bags once and for all. Sven, her husband, was supposed to be working away that day and I was going to pick her and her daughter up later with their bags.' She bit her lower lip and shook her head. 'But somehow I had a really bad feeling about it, so I went along earlier to help her pack. And when I got to their apartment, it turned out he was already there. He flipped when he found out that she wanted to leave him – he lost it, worse than ever before. When I heard the screams, I ran straight into the apartment.' She shook her head again. 'He hadn't even bothered to shut the door.' Lena felt her eyes well up and she forced herself to fight the tears. 'My sister was sitting under the kitchen table, covered in blood, crying her eyes out. I tried to calm her, and suddenly we heard Fabienne screaming from the living room.' Lena swallowed. 'We both jumped up and ran in there straight away. Sven was about to let rip on the little girl when Tamara grabbed a trophy from the shelf and smashed it down on his head.' As Lena talked, she pictured everything as clearly as though it were yesterday. 'When the police arrived, Sven was already dead.'

Stunned, Belling shook his head. 'Was . . . was she sentenced?'

Lena nodded, as if in slow motion. 'Although she acted in self-defence, Tamara was still sentenced to two years in prison . . . That's a long time, especially if you have a small child.'

He nodded, distressed by the story. 'My God, I . . . I had no idea.'

62

But Lena's story was far from over. 'At that time I blamed myself for having abandoned my sister all those years.'

He looked at her. 'But you tried again and again to help her.'

'But there was so much more I could have done!' The despair she felt back then was clear from her expression. 'And then, the day before she was put away, I finally made the decision that Fabienne shouldn't grow up without her biological mother.'

He frowned. 'What do you mean?'

Lena fixed her gaze on his face. 'As you know, Tamara and I are identical twins. Sometimes even our parents weren't a hundred percent sure which of us was which.' She looked around to make sure no one was listening before she carried on. 'On the morning her sentence was due to commence, I was the one who walked through the gates into the women's prison. I . . . I pretended to be my twin sister and served her prison sentence on her behalf.'

Completely speechless, Belling stared at her, his mouth slightly open for a second while he tried to process what Lena had just confided in him.

'I . . . I don't know what to say,' he gasped, still quite perplexed.

There was silence for a moment. Still dwelling on her thoughts, Lena put the sugar dispenser back on the counter.

She had read whatever books on criminology she could get her hands on back then. And if her time behind bars had done any good at all, it was that she had been able to study her fellow inmates from close up, analysing their thinking and behaviour, and thereby gathering unique insider knowledge as a criminal profiler.

'That . . . that was pretty selfless of you,' Belling said to break the silence and looked at her with a warm expression. 'Blimey, Peters, you're not a bad egg.'

Lena smiled and felt herself blush. But her smile was quick to vanish. 'But not a word to anyone, OK?' she whispered, bending forwards slightly. 'If the fact that I've been in prison ever comes out, I'll lose my licence.'

'Uh, yes, of course. My lips are sealed.'

She smiled. Wulf Belling might have his flaws, but his heart was in the right place. Besides, he seemed a man of his word and Lena felt quite sure that her secret was safe with him. She drank her espresso, which had gone cold in the meantime, and was just about to put the cup down on the saucer when Belling's mobile rang.

'That'll be Tamara,' he said, relieved. With the words, 'It wouldn't surprise me if she's waiting outside my front door because she can't get in,' he answered the phone.

Then all colour drained from his face. He stared wide-eyed at Lena as his lips silently uttered a name. Lena understood: *Artifex*.

63

Lena jumped up and stood as close as she could to Belling to listen in to the conversation. 'What do you want?' Belling asked.

'Have you seen your little friend in the last twenty-four hours?' It was the same voice – disguised by a vocoder.

'What . . . what do you mean?'

Suddenly they heard stifled screams down the phone line. Belling and Lena looked at each other. The same thought flashed through both of their heads: *Tamara! And the baby!*

Lena felt like her heart had stopped. And as she tried to fight the mounting panic attack, the crowded cafe with all the waitresses and the clatter of cutlery seemed a million miles away all of a sudden.

'For heaven's sake! Let them go!' Belling's voice trembled.

They heard a disdainful laugh.

'My God, at least let the baby go!' Belling did not want to give up.

'I want fifty thousand euros, cash. Bring the money in a plastic bag to the old slaughterhouse in Lichterfelde and leave it in the old stables. You'll find an envelope next to the feed troughs with the address of where you'll find your little friend and the baby.'

Belling looked at Lena as he clutched the phone so tightly that his knuckles were almost white.

'In three hours,' the voice commanded. 'Come alone. If you don't, the woman and baby die.'

A click. The caller had hung up.

Belling dropped his hand holding the phone and stared at Lena for a moment, his eyes wide. Both had a look of sheer horror.

'What are you doing?' asked Belling, as Lena took the phone out of his hand and started dialling a number.

'I'm telling Volker Drescher.'

Belling looked at her with pursed lips. 'Are you sure? I mean, it wouldn't be the first time Drescher and his inept team—'

'Am I sure?' Lena interrupted him forcefully. She pointed with an outstretched arm to the door. 'My twin sister is out there with her seven-month-old baby in the hands of a brutal serial killer and you ask me if I'm sure?!'

Belling swallowed and suddenly realised that pretty much every pair of eyes in the cafe were on them.

'It may be that you think we can solve this case on our own, but I . . .' she said, slapping the palm of her hand against her chest, 'I'm not going to put Tamara and the baby at risk by trying to go it alone.'

In a fury, Lena ran out of the cafe with the phone, without paying the slightest bit of notice to the attention she had attracted.

64

'I'm sorry, I didn't mean to shout at you,' Lena said a little later when she was sitting in Belling's passenger seat, still in a daze.

'No, I'm the one who should apologise – you're right.' He put his hand on Lena's slender shoulder and looked at her intently.

He started the engine of his Peugeot and set off for the homicide division. After Lena had told Volker Drescher on the phone what had happened, he reproached her bitterly for pursuing the case further without his knowledge. He ordered her to come to the bureau immediately, while he assembled a Special Forces team at top speed and got the fifty thousand euros in cash ready for the ransom. Lena looked anxiously at her watch. They had exactly two hours and fifty-one minutes to work out a strategy that, at the handover, would be a matter of life or death. Lena knew only too well what dangers lurked in a high-risk operation of this kind, which so often went wrong. It was all the more important now to make use of all her professionalism and her strategic skills, rather than letting herself be guided by her feelings. Still, she wondered what Artifex was doing asking for a ransom. With serial killers it was never about the money, that much was clear. For a moment she asked herself if they were dealing with a copycat. But how would he know Artifex's name?

Lena wiped the tears from her cheek as Belling stopped the car. Confused, she looked out the window and then at Belling when she realised that they were at her apartment. 'Why are we here?'

'Has it occurred to you that the killer might have confused your sister for you?'

Lena sat up in her seat. 'Yes . . . it's possible. But what are you getting at?'

Belling nodded to her flat. 'Go and get the pistol – you should at least have it with you now.'

Lena stared at him. But this time she did not disagree. She got out and went to fetch the gun, while Belling remained seated in the car and waited for her.

65

Lena rushed through the courtyard to her apartment and cursed her tears, which were now freely running down her cheeks. *Pull yourself together, damn it! It won't help Tamara and Marcel if you lose your nerve now.*

With trembling hands she unlocked the front door and went straight to the bedroom. She squatted down in front of the dresser and rifled through her underwear and pyjamas in the bottom drawer looking for the gun. 'Come on, where are you hiding?' She was hastily ransacking the drawer when she heard a faint clicking sound and sensed someone behind her.

'Hello, Lena,' she heard a voice say. Lena gasped. She straightened up and slowly turned around. Frozen, she looked into the blue eyes of the man who was now standing in her bedroom doorway holding her cat under his arm. In the other hand he held her gun.

'Is this what you're looking for?' With a jovial grin he brandished the pistol in the air. 'And I thought I was going to have to wait here all day for you, my dear little Lena.'

She winced and felt the fine hairs on her neck stand on end as she realised who was standing there in front of her. Artifex.

'How did you get into my apartment?'

He laughed mockingly, as though he took the question as an insult. And after a glance at the open French doors, Lena knew the answer.

The man put Napoleon down, who immediately scarpered with a meow.

Lena's heart was pounding. 'My partner's waiting outside in the car. If I'm not back in a minute, he'll come and look for me.'

Seemingly unimpressed, Artifex started to walk towards her. Lena held her breath and stepped back towards the bed. The man was a good two heads taller than her. If she could just get hold of the knife that she had tucked under the mattress, then she might have a realistic chance against him. With the pistol in his hand he came close towards her – he was now just a few steps away. When Lena finally reached the foot of the bed, he laughed again.

'That's a bad idea,' he muttered, shaking his head. He reached into the back pocket of his jeans and pulled out the knife – the one she'd been hoping to find. Lena felt a lump in her throat. Not only did he look physically stronger than her, but he now had a deadly weapon in each hand. She was trapped. She had no choice but to play the only card she had. She swerved and ran like lightning. But he was faster. Artifex grabbed her by the hair. He yanked her back and flung her on the bed. The sharp blade of the knife caught her on the cheek. A burning pain shot through Lena's face and a surge of warm blood flowed from the gash down her neck. Just as the man lunged at her, Lena rolled herself up on her back and gave him a hefty kick. He staggered backwards and fell against the bedroom mirror. The glass broke into thousands of pieces. The gun fell to the floor and slid under the wardrobe. Giddy for a moment, Artifex held his head, and Lena managed to make a dash for the corridor.

'Stop, you bitch!' she heard him call from the bedroom while she paced madly down the hall to the front door.

66

She had almost reached the door when she suddenly felt an unbelievable stinging pain that shot up her left leg from the back of her calf. Lena fell to the ground, groaning and writhing in agony. Her eyes darted to the knife, which he had thrown at her and which was deep in her calf. She gritted her teeth and yanked it out of the flesh. The blood poured from under her jeans down to her ankle and dripped onto the floorboards, while for a moment her vision went black. Gritting her teeth against the pain, Lena pulled herself up and limped as fast as she could towards the door. *Faster, run faster!* But before she knew it, Artifex had caught up with her. He forced her to the ground again, while Lena lashed out wildly, desperately, fiercely with the bloody knife in her hand. But Artifex kicked it out of her grasp. Lena was lying on her stomach, trying to crawl towards the door, when he threw himself onto his knees on her back. Lena felt like she might suffocate under his weight, when she suddenly saw that he had a syringe in his hand, which was in front of her, pinning her down. At that moment she heard the buzz of the doorbell. She stared wide-eyed at the door. *Belling!* He was there, just a few metres away. Lena wanted to scream and attract his attention, but Artifex had one hand over her mouth and with the other he squeezed the syringe against her neck.

'One peep and I'll inject,' he breathed quietly into her ear, leaning so close that she could feel his breath. With the sharp needle against her neck, she breathed heavily through her nose, in and out, and did not dare move.

The doorbell rang again. Then Belling knocked on the door. 'Peters? Everything OK?'

Sweat streamed from Lena's pores, she could hardly breathe. And then suddenly Artifex injected her. Lena's screams were muffled by his strong hand. After a brief moment she felt her limbs go limp. She fought it with all her strength, but her muscles refused to respond. Her mouth felt numb; she was paralysed. Artifex heaved her up like a wet sack. And while Lena could only just, with great difficulty, keep her eyes open, she registered that he was dragging her through the back door and out onto the patio.

67

Two hours later

The rain slithered in thin trickles across the windshield as Wulf Belling sat behind the wheel of his car, a cigarette in his mouth, driving aimlessly through the streets. He could still hardly believe what had just happened, and the events of the last few hours ran through his mind again and again like a film on fast-forward. When Lena Peters didn't open the door, he got anxious. He rang the doorbell several times and when, shortly afterwards, she still hadn't appeared, he unceremoniously battered down the door only to discover the bloodstains on the floorboards, at which point he ran crazily through the apartment. But all he found was the open patio door. It was barely a quarter of an hour after his call to the homicide division when Volker Drescher arrived with his team. The forensics team had the whole apartment turned upside down, but not a single clue was found that hinted at where Lena Peters had been taken. Equally disappointing was how the ransom payment had turned out. Belling had been more than willing to do the handover himself. He would have gladly offered to wire himself up and take the goddamn plastic bag full of money into the slaughterhouse; he would have put his life at stake without batting an eyelid.

However, after the second sister had been kidnapped, Drescher would no longer listen to reason. The head of Homicide was firmly convinced that Belling had already done enough damage and instructed him to stay out of the investigation once and for all. He even reserved the right to pursue criminal penalties. Just the thought of how Drescher's stubborn adherence to the rules had contributed to the failure of the ransom drop filled Belling with immense fury. Because, as he learned shortly afterwards, when Drescher's people got access to the stables, instead of an address, they found only an empty envelope. And while the kidnapper did a runner with the ransom, Tamara and baby Marcel were still missing without a trace. Shaking his head, Belling drove on and on while the windscreen wipers struggled against the pounding rain. He put out his cigarette in the ashtray in the centre console and his mournful eyes wandered involuntarily to the empty passenger seat. He should never have let Peters go into her apartment by herself! Plagued by guilt, he prayed to God that she was still alive. And Tamara and the baby. It was driving him crazy, knowing they were at the mercy of this brutal serial killer and that there was nothing he could do. He decided he would stop by the gallery of this Oleg. That was the only thing left that he could do.

Belling stopped at a red light and took his packet of cigarettes out of his side pocket, only to find that it was already empty. He stopped at a kiosk just ten minutes away from his house and bought another packet. He put the change back in his pocket and was about to walk back to his car when a woman caught his eye: she had just dashed out of the Woolworth's on the other side of the road and sprinted into the pedestrian area. She was wearing a short denim skirt and a blouse, and had light brown hair twisted into a slightly dishevelled bun. Her face was hidden behind black sunglasses, but Belling was pretty certain that it was Tamara. But how could that be?

68

Wulf Belling could hardly believe his eyes. The woman was off at full pelt.

'Hey, wait! Stop!' he shouted and ran across the street, paying no attention to the traffic, hurrying after her through the busy pedestrian street. She then sped up and Belling struggled to catch up with her. Since he had started smoking again, his lungs were giving him more and more trouble. Panting heavily, he dashed through the crowd, swerving like a slalom skier around mothers pushing buggies, loitering teenagers and shoppers laden with bags strolling through the precinct.

'Hey, fatso, look where you're going!' shouted one man who, jostled by Belling, had dropped his curry wurst. When Belling was just an arm's length from the woman, he grabbed her by the jacket and held her tight. She writhed under his grip and tried to pull away. Belling dragged her back and an armful of bracelets and earrings, still with their price tags on, fell jingling onto the cobbled street.

'Hey, man, what the fuck? You're playing at being a store detective now?'

Belling stared at her face. Although he was angry with her, he also never dreamed he would be so glad to see Tamara.

'I thought you were long—' he began, as relieved as he was stunned.

She pushed her sunglasses up her nose. 'Thought I was what?' she asked, looking at him defiantly.

He looked around. 'Where's Marcel?'

'With a girlfriend. What's it to you?'

He looked confused. 'I thought you didn't know anyone in Berlin?'

'Who says?' She spat her gum out. 'I'll tell you something: unlike my sister, I have friends everywhere! And besides, it's got nothing to do with you.' Huffing and puffing, she bent down to pick up the stolen jewellery. Belling still stared at her, perplexed. Tamara appeared to have no idea about what had happened that afternoon. And gradually it dawned on Belling: the killer had been able to pick up the ransom at the same time as kidnapping Lena Peters from her apartment because Artifex and the black-mailer who had phoned Belling were two different people. But as the blackmailer had called himself Artifex on the phone – a name that had never emerged in the press – they had naturally assumed that it was in fact the infamous Mutilator. But whoever the caller was, he had been bluffing from the outset. At least some of this was starting to make more sense. But if the caller was not the serial killer they were after, then who was he? As much as he racked his brains, Belling had not the foggiest idea.

'Wait, I'll help you.' He scooped up a pair of earrings and handed them to her.

Tamara looked up, confused, and shook her head. 'I don't get you at all. First you chase me down half the shopping precinct because of a bit of tat and then you don't even want me to return it?'

Belling looked at her pityingly. She really had not the slight-est clue about what had happened. He took a moment to answer and felt a huge lump in his throat. He would have to tell her.

69

Spandau, Berlin

Lena felt like she was suffocating from the tape over her mouth. She was lying on an operating table, strapped down by her arms and legs. She had nothing on but a hospital gown. She squinted at the dazzling lights that were directed straight at her face, while her eyes searched for a way out. It took great effort to raise her head even the tiniest amount. The room was strangely blurred. Everything was spinning. Next to a solid steel door less than two metres away, she could see the contours of a motionless figure sitting there, which had a sheet draped over it. From the shape it looked like a woman.

'Hello, little Lena,' came Artifex's now familiar voice. Lena winced; a shiver ran through her. He had been standing behind her the whole time, watching her. He walked over to the operating table, wearing light green hospital scrubs, a cap and a mask. His piercing blue eyes gazed at her. 'I hope you're on good form, because today's your big day.' He yanked the wide strip of tape off her mouth. 'I don't think you need that any more. You're not likely to be able to speak right now anyway. But don't worry, you don't need to say anything – it's enough for you just to feel what I'm going to do to you.' He grinned again. 'After all, you're finally going to have a proper role in this when a part of you is immortalised in my masterpiece.'

Lena stared at him with hateful eyes. The alcuronium chloride. He must have already injected her with it. He opened her mouth and rammed a tube down her throat, which was linked up to a ventilator. The action was so rough and sudden that Lena felt like he had rammed a knife down her throat. It was extremely painful.

'Have you ever stuffed an animal, little Lena?' She watched as he picked up a cotton wool ball and doused it with disinfectant.

'No? Too bad. Somehow I thought you had the same ambitions as me as a child. You ought to know: you and I, my dear Lena, we're not so different.'

The next thing she knew, he was wiping her eyelids with the cotton swab. The disinfectant burned the delicate skin and her eyes welled up with tears. When her field of vision had cleared enough, she saw that he had pulled on a pair of latex gloves.

'I had a good little look around at your place. A nice apartment. And all those lovely photos of the mutilated women. I could hardly decorate my own flat better myself.' He looked at her for a moment and ran the back of his hand across her cheek before he asked, 'How are you with pain, little Lena?'

She saw that he was bending down over her. His hand was approaching her face. Then he pulled her lower eyelid down with his thumb and shone a narrow medical torch directly into her eye, so that the pupil contracted.

'Your light green eyes have always fascinated me – did you know that, little Lena? Ever since I first saw you at our swimming lessons.'

Swimming lessons? *My God, who is this man?* Feverishly she searched through her memory, while noticing that his eyes kept flitting over to the figure by the door. It was as if he was under observation and needed the tacit consent of this person before he could proceed.

'I was a few years above you.' He laughed. 'But I was at least a head shorter than everyone else. I was the little boy who was always scared of going in the deep pool. Do you remember now?'

Thoughts and memories raced through Lena's head and suddenly it occurred to her: Viktor Rudolf! Even way back then, the boy stood out as being a bit odd. Lena remembered that after his parents had died, he lived with his older sister Mathilda, whom he really idolised. They lived just a few streets away and in Fischbach everyone knew each other. It was said that the boy had stuffed his little terrier to preserve him for ever. Lena never paid much attention to the rumours. Not even when Viktor Rudolf's sister became ill all of a sudden and from one day to the next was mysteriously bedridden. There was the wildest speculation about what was wrong with her, since nobody ever saw her again in the flesh. Her gaze inevitably flitted back to the sheet-covered figure and an awful thought occurred to her. *Oh God!*

'So I was all the more delighted to see you again in Berlin,' Viktor Rudolf continued calmly, moving away from the operating table. 'Just as with our mutual acquaintance, Suzanna Wirt.'

Gradually, it all started to fall into place. That was how he knew about her parents' tragic accident.

Artifex went on to tell her about how his seventeen-year-old sister Tilla had already taken over most of the important roles in the household, even when their parents were still alive. She was seen as responsible and trustworthy and the youth welfare office had agreed that, under strict conditions, the siblings could carry on living in their parents' house, which saved them having to be put in a children's home or placed with foster families.

Looking back, Artifex could safely say that the time he spent in that house with Tilla after his parents' death was the loveliest time of his life. That was until the day that Tilla introduced him to Vincent Rothenbaum. Vincent was twice as old as Tilla and, right from the start, he was a thorn in the side of the then fifteen-year-old Artifex. Although Artifex did succeed in coming between them, his life soon took another dramatic turn. Tilla got the idea of finding a flat of her own. No sooner had she announced the devastating news than a violent quarrel ensued between the two siblings, which resulted in Tilla falling down the stairs and being fatally injured. Artifex's life fell apart. In desperation, the teen, who was already very interested in medicine and who always used to look over the shoulder of his thanatologist father, managed to cover up his beloved sister's death and left no stone unturned in his effort to preserve her body. He had still, to this very day, not tired of finding ways to improve Tilla, his first preserved body. Now all he needed to finish his masterpiece was to add the crucial final ingredient. Lena heard him opening a drawer. No more than twenty seconds later, he was back at the operating table. Her gaze was transfixed by the scalpel in his hand.

'Are you ready?'

Lena felt nauseous when she saw the scalpel approaching her face.

He pushed her eyelids apart with his gloved fingers. Then he leaned down to her and whispered, 'Your eyes are mine.'

70

Wulf Belling parked his Peugeot on Kottbusser Tor. He walked down the street towards Oleg Semak's gallery as a cool breeze whistled through his hair. After he had filled Tamara in on events, she completely freaked out. It was almost impossible to reassure her. He had dropped her off at the police headquarters, mainly to prevent her from doing anything stupid. He had then set off straight away for Kreuzberg. Belling pulled his jacket zip up and had another glance around him. It wasn't long until he stopped in front of a rundown shop front, where the initials O.S. were written on the door. Oleg Semak. The door was locked. Belling took a step back and looked up at the façade, which was sprayed with graffiti. Lena was right: if you weren't a regular customer, you would have no idea that there was a gallery here. He went up to the window and used his hand to shield his eyes from the light. Behind the glass lay a mostly empty room with just a ladder, an upturned paint pot and some plaster sculptures. Belling's eyes fell on the staircase at the far end of the room, leading down to the basement. He reached into his jacket pocket and as he looked at the small, hooked lock-picking tool he always carried with him, he hesitated. After all, from what Lena said, this Semak and his associates were not to be messed with. If they caught him snooping down there, he would be up shit creek. But

Belling saw no other way. Determined to go ahead, he glanced over his shoulder and fumbled with the lock. No sooner had the door sprung open, than Belling entered and headed for the stairs. Cautiously, he climbed down the steps, which brought him down to a dark cellar. As he reached the bottom, he was hit by the pungent stench of strong chemicals. Belling looked around for a light switch on the wall. There didn't seem to be one. Slowly he groped his way forwards into the room. It took a while for his eyes to get used to the dark. Gradually, all around him he started to see the contours of life-size figures. Belling pulled his cigarette lighter out of his pocket and shone it about. A lump came to his throat when, in the faint light given off by the flame, he saw himself surrounded by human specimens, animal heads and other strange, distorted creatures. Belling forced himself to keep looking around, to identify anything that might indicate the name of the creator. But besides price tags, which listed astonishingly high prices in yen, dollars and rubles, he could see nothing that might shed light on who this alleged 'artist' was. He was almost certain that his visit was in vain when he spotted a piece of paper stuck to a shelf full of packing material. He pulled off the piece of paper and scanned the address written on it.

'In Spandau . . .' murmured Belling. He stuck it in his pocket, then all of a sudden he heard noises coming from the ground floor. Men, speaking in Russian.

Damn it! As fast as he could, Belling dashed back to the stairs. He held his breath when he saw a man of medium build coming down the steps with two giants in tow. He spun around in a panic, looking for somewhere to hide.

'Just one more little thing, then we can get going,' Lena heard Artifex say and saw him move away from the operating table again. 'Don't run away, I'll be right back.'

His laughter echoed through the room. Moments later, she could hear Verdi's 'La Traviata'.

The opera that Christine Wagenbach mentioned, thought Lena, remembering only too well what a horrifying ordeal Wagenbach had been subjected to.

And now it was her.

Tears ran down her face as Artifex reappeared beside the operating table with a scalpel in hand.

'You've gone quite pale with fear.' He sounded genuinely concerned. 'But there's no need,' he said, gently stroking a strand of hair from her forehead that was damp with sweat. 'In my experience it only hurts at first. I admit that the procedure is complicated and it might take as long as several hours but, trust me, once the first eyeball is removed, the pain will be so unbearable that with any luck you'll soon lose consciousness.'

Lena waited for him to insert the scalpel.

As fast as he could, Wulf Belling darted behind one of the specimens. Suddenly the neon ceiling lights burst into action. It was less than five seconds before the Russians discovered him. Belling saw them look at each other with fury in their eyes.

'Look here – we've got a visitor!' A dark-haired, pale-skinned man with a ponytail and a thin goatee stepped towards him with an insidious grin.

Oleg Semak – that had to be him, thought Belling as he spotted the skull tattoo on the man's throat.

'Do we like uninvited guests?' he asked, turning to his men.

The two giants shook their heads. Belling felt the cold fear in his chest and already knew full well what was coming. Semak's face contorted into an ugly grimace.

'And what do we do with uninvited guests?'

Sweat gathered on Belling's forehead when he saw the giants walking slowly towards him with their arms crossed.

'Guys, we can talk about this!' Defensively he stretched his palms out towards them and tried to smile, while he looked around in panic for the nearest object he could grab. But there was nothing that he could use as a weapon. He felt himself go hot and cold at the same time when he saw one of the two thugs grabbing a heavy crowbar and swinging it in his hand like a baseball bat, while the other one pulled out a knuckle-duster.

'Wait, I . . . I'm police!' He stepped back until he was standing with his back to the wall.

Suddenly he saw the Russian raise his arm to strike. Belling ducked. The crowbar struck him on the back of his head. He fell to the ground and his face smashed against the floor. Gasping with pain, he reached up to his head. Then, dizzy, he straightened up, went onto all fours and tried to get up. But when he went to raise his head, the Russian kicked him back to the ground. Again and again, the boot smashed into his face. Belling tried to protect his face with his hands, but heard his jawbone crack. The pain was so brutal that soon he could do nothing other than just lie there. When the Russians finally relented, he strained to open his swollen eyelids. He spat out a tooth and was startled when he saw all the blood on the floor. His blood. Belling whimpered desperately, begging for mercy.

Oleg Semak came towards him with a condescending grin. He ran his hand under Belling's bloody chin and raised his head until Belling was looking him in the eye. 'But we have only just begun.'

Belling felt giddy when he saw Semak step back and pick the crowbar up from the ground.

It was at this moment that he wished he was already dead.

73

Lena felt him press the blade slightly down into the delicate skin below her right eye. A sharp pain rushed in, along with the blood, which oozed along her cheekbone like a thick caterpillar. Lena had already resigned herself to the fact that she was going to die in this cellar when suddenly she heard something. The sound of voices through the cellar walls. Dogs barking. Lena's eyes widened. Police dogs. Artifex also heard it. He stopped mid-motion and looked up aghast.

'No, that can't be!' He put the scalpel down on the tray of surgical instruments and walked over to the massive metal door. He put an ear against the smooth steel surface, as if to make sure that he hadn't just imagined the noises. But when the siren sounded, Lena saw from his face that he also understood.

They had found her.

She felt a flicker of hope that she might still get out of there alive. Artifex gave her a strange look, but nothing in his face revealed what he was thinking. Then he turned his gaze to the figure by the door. He ran his hand gently over the sheet and said, 'Don't worry, Tilla, the door is made of reinforced steel. We're as safe here as in Fort Knox. Nothing and no one is going to stop me from completing my masterpiece.'

HANNA WINTER | 251

'This is the police! Open the door immediately and leave the room with your hands up!' came the amplified voice, muffled by the door.

Lena recognised the voice of Volker Drescher.

'Open the door! This is the final call!'

Suddenly she could hear the dull blows of a battering ram and the scratching sound of a crowbar trying to break through the steel frame.

The Special Forces are trying to storm the room. But Lena's relief was short-lived. When she saw that the door stood unmoved despite all the attempts to open it, hope left her.

74

Lena realised that she was trapped in a huge, utterly impenetrable vault. The only difference was that down here all she would find was death – not gold bullion. Artifex turned the opera up as loud as it would go and walked back over to her. He calmly picked the scalpel up again. Beads of sweat ran down Lena's temples when he appeared just above her, grinning in anticipation. One last glance over at the shrouded figure, then he inserted the scalpel again where he had left off. Lena forced herself not to look at him, and for a moment she did not know what was worse: her helplessness in his hands or her imminent fate that she now knew was inevitable. Had she been able to, she would have screamed for her life.

There was a deafening bang. Lena was stunned by the force of the explosion, which was so great that the figure by the door was shredded into thousands of pieces. A dense surge of smoke veiled the room. A monotonous beep buzzed in Lena's ear and she could just about make out Artifex. He had been hurled against the wall by the force of the detonation and now he reeled in horror at the sight of his ruined work of art.

'Nooooo! Tilla!' he shouted in despair. Torches shone through the smoke and focussed on his face. Within seconds, the fire – fuelled by the tanks of chemicals – reached the operating room. Lena lay panting heavily, still motionless on the table. The smoke was now so thick that it was making it almost impossible to see – or breathe. Commands were shouted. Shots echoed through the room, and she could only just about make out Artifex, his chest pierced by bullets, falling to the ground beside her. Lena was unable to move – just like the time she was trapped in the burning car with her parents. And as the paramedics and firefighters in their gas masks drew closer, recurring scenes from that day played out in her mind. But her guardian angel still did not abandon her. Just like that time, the emergency services arrived to rescue her seconds before she lost consciousness.

75

Four days later

Lena walked along the hospital corridor with a bouquet of flowers and a box of chocolates, heading for Wulf Belling's room. While Lena had got away with a serious shock and a small cut under her right eye, Belling was lucky to still be alive. A jogger had found him in the woods just in time. If he had been found just a few hours later, the doctors said he would have succumbed to his injuries. Lena opened the door to Belling's room, bracing herself for barely recognising him after everything that had happened to him.

But when she peered into the room his bed was empty. Lena did not move a muscle, staring for a second at the empty bed. Suddenly the tears welled up in her eyes. She was too late. She had not even been able to say goodbye to him. She let the chocolates and the flowers fall to the floor, put her hands to her mouth and began to cry bitterly.

'Now, now – who's that crying?' she heard a weak-sounding voice behind her.

Lena looked up. When she turned around, she was looking into the eyes of Wulf Belling, who was standing there on crutches with a bandaged head, a leg in plaster and a bandaged arm. His face looked as if he had left a boxing match behind him. One that he had lost hands down.

'Belling.'

He smiled. 'You disappoint me, Peters – did you really think I'd go without a fight?'

She was overjoyed to see him and would have gladly thrown her arms around him. Again her tears welled up. But this time they were tears of joy.

'Admit it – you were worried about me,' he murmured.

'Me? Never!' Lena replied jokingly and beamed at him. Then she picked the flowers and chocolates up from the floor.

'Are they for me?'

She nodded. 'How are you?'

Belling laughed. 'As you can see – fabulous. And you?'

Lena's lips curled into a smile again while she pointed her finger at her eyes. 'As you can see, my eyes are still *in situ*.'

Belling laughed wheezily. 'Stop it! It hurts like hell when you make me laugh . . . Come on, I've been moved to the next room.' Still a little shaky, he hobbled forwards on his crutches.

Lena followed him and held the door open for him. No sooner had the door to his room closed behind them, than Belling told her what had happened to him in the gallery.

'I have absolutely no memory of them sticking me in their car and kicking me out God knows where in the suburbs. I must have been delirious,' he said as he lay back down in bed. 'It was pure chance that a jogger passed by and found me.'

Still bewildered, Lena, who had sat down on a chair beside his bed, shook her head. 'And when you came round in the hospital and told the police about the Russians and the preserved human bodies, Volker Drescher stormed the basement of the gallery right away.' She shook her head again. 'I dread to think what would have happened if he hadn't found the piece of paper with the address of Artifex's workshop down there . . .'

Belling looked up, puzzled. 'He found the address?'

'Uh, yes – at least that's what he said.'

'That's interesting . . .' Belling sat up awkwardly in bed. He reached with his good hand in the drawer of the bedside table and pulled out a clear plastic bag containing a blood-soaked piece of paper with a handwritten address on it. 'I guess you mean this? The note was forwarded to Homicide after I arrived at the emergency room.'

Lena looked at him speechless. 'Tsh, that's just typical.'

He made a gesture of indifference. 'What the heck – let's let Drescher have his little bit of ill-gotten kudos.'

They laughed. At that moment there was a knock at the door. Belling put the bag back in the drawer.

'Come in.'

The door opened, and to both of their surprise Tamara entered the room with baby Marcel in her arms. 'I just wanted to say goodbye.' She looked alternately at Lena and Belling as she approached the bed. 'I've found a new job and it starts tomorrow.'

Lena's mouth turned up into a smile. 'That's great news.'

Tamara nodded and wiped her runny nose with the back of her hand. 'And . . . Well, I wanted to say that I'm sorry. I've not been on my best behaviour, I realise that now.'

Belling smiled.

'Perhaps you'll come and visit me again,' said Lena, stroking little Marcel tenderly on his head.

'Yes, definitely . . .' Tamara smiled.

If she had not been standing with her back to Belling, she might have seen him gesture to Lena by pulling his finger across his neck. Lena had to smile. They said goodbye to Tamara and watched as she and the baby disappeared through the door, just as Volker Drescher came in.

'I hope I'm not disturbing you.'

Belling grinned. 'Come in.'

Drescher pushed his glasses back into place and said, 'I just wanted to let you know that Oleg Semak and his men were caught last night. We have been observing the gang for some time, but have never been able to prove anything. But with your statement and everything that's come to light in the basement of this alleged gallery, they won't be out for a while.'

Belling nodded slowly. 'I hope so.'

'Yes, well, that was what I wanted to tell you,' Drescher concluded and turned to Lena. 'So, will I see you on Monday at the police station?'

She smiled, surprised, and looked at him for a moment, thinking. 'Only under the condition that I choose my own partner,' she said, nodding at Wulf Belling.

But Drescher seemed far from pleased. He stood with his arms crossed at the foot of the bed and was about to say something when Lena forestalled him.

'After all, it is thanks to Belling that you were able to make the connection to the killer.'

Drescher turned red and looked at Lena and Belling alternately. 'So now you only come as a double act, huh?'

Lena and Belling smiled at each other conspiratorially. They were an unbeatable team – that much was clear.

'All right,' said Drescher, grudgingly. 'If that's how it is, I hardly have any choice.' He took a deep breath and turned to face Belling. 'Once you're back on your feet, come and see me at my office . . . But I'll tell you this once, Belling: if you screw up, you're straight back out again.'

Belling nodded. 'Oh, Herr Drescher?' he called when the head of Homicide was already at the door.

Drescher stopped and turned to face him. 'Yes?'

'The mysterious caller who posed as Artifex – do we know yet who that was?'

'As a matter of fact, yes. It was a junkie called Gemmy. The boy knew Artifex, and when he discovered what was going on in the basement workshop he saw the picture of Frau Peters and got the blackmail idea. He probably assumed that she was already in Artifex's hands.'

'And how do you know all this?' asked Lena.

'Because this Gemmy was caught driving a stolen car later on the night of the handover, with the ransom money in the boot. My guys only had to cross-examine him for so long before he sang.'

'But the muffled screams on the phone . . . ?' Lena threw in.

'A DVD he was playing in the background,' Drescher reported. He laughed, shaking his head. 'Gemmy didn't know about your twin sister or the baby.'

'But one thing I can't make sense of,' Belling joined in. 'How did this brat get my phone number?'

Drescher shoved his glasses back into place with his index finger. 'Initially he only had Frau Peters' number from the photo in the basement, but it was useless after her phone was stolen, so he started spying on her. That must have been when he got onto you. And he got your number from the internet somehow. This

Gemmy had planned everything to the last detail. He even got hold of a vocoder like the one Artifex used for his phone calls.'

'I had a feeling from the start that the call was from someone else,' agreed Lena.

'Really? What made you think that?' Belling wanted to know.

Lena looked at him. 'Apart from the fact that blackmail doesn't fit into our serial killer's profile, what I realised later on was that when Artifex rang me he addressed me as "du", but this guy was more formal and addressed you as "Sie".'

Belling nodded approvingly. 'Not bad, partner.'

Drescher coughed loudly. 'OK, see you soon, then,' he said and left the room.

Barely a minute passed after Volker Drescher left before there was a knock at the door again.

'Marietta – wow, you're the last person I expected to see after my embarrassing appearance the other day!' blurted Belling when his daughter walked in through the door.

'Hey, Dad, I'm so sorry for everything,' she said ruefully, sitting down on the bed next to her father.

Belling introduced Marietta and Lena. But Lena had the feeling that father and daughter had a lot to say to each other and pushed her chair back to stand up.

'The other night, you weren't the only one who had trouble getting home . . .' Marietta confessed.

'What do you mean?' Belling asked.

'Well, what can I say . . . I lost my wallet in the club. It must have fallen out of my pocket somehow while I was dancing. So I had no money for a taxi.'

'And those guys you were with didn't give you a lift?'

She shook her head.

Belling looked at her, worried. 'Why not?'

'Oh, we had an argument. And at some point they just vanished.' She reached for his hand. 'Dad, I'm so sorry for what I said – I didn't mean it.'

His face softened straight away into a gentle smile. 'Come here, you. It's long forgotten.'

With tears in her eyes, Marietta laid her head on his chest. Lena looked at them both. Although with his multiple fractures he had probably never been in such a bad state, she had also never seen Wulf Belling as happy as at that moment. Lena got the feeling that she was not needed, so she got up and walked slowly over to the door.

'I think I'd better go then.' She cleared her throat and left the two of them alone.

76

The next morning

Still breathless from jogging, Lena reached her house and went to open the mailbox. Advertising flyers, letters and two slim packages. Back in her apartment, she kicked her trainers off in the hall and walked into the kitchen. She placed the mail on the table and put some coffee on. She drank a large glass of tap water, and while the coffee machine was softly humming to itself, she started looking through the mail. Curious, she opened the larger of the two parcels first. Inside was a chess computer – the latest generation with various difficulty levels and all kinds of features. Lena was delighted. On the card enclosed, she read:

So you don't always have to play against yourself.
Best regards, Volker Drescher

Lena laughed and shook her head. But she was glad to accept his effort at reconciliation.

Then she ripped open the smaller packet. It was a new notebook. Another present that could not have been more appropriate.

'A new case, a new notebook,' she said to herself cheerfully. She ran her thumb over the leather cover and flicked through the pages, wondering who had sent it. There didn't seem to be a card enclosed. But it was certainly someone who had been very attentive. Perhaps Belling. Or Lukas? Lena smiled as she thought about what she could do to pay Lukas back for his help in finding Cornelia Dobelli. Perhaps she would ask him to the cinema. She was just about to close the book when she paused. Her cheerful mood vanished abruptly. The last page of the notebook had a message written on it. Blood-red handwriting that read:

Do what I say.
Or I'll kill you.

About the Author

Hanna Winter lives in New York and works as a freelance writer. Her first thriller, *The Children's Trail*, was published in 2010 and became an instant bestseller in Germany.

The serial killer thriller that took Europe by storm – out now in paperback

Turn the page for an exclusive first look . . .

Prologue

West Berlin – 13 October, 11.09 p.m.

Gabriel stood in the doorway and stared. The light from the hall fell down the cellar stairs and was swallowed by the brick walls.

He hated the cellar, particularly at night. Not that it would've made any difference whether it was light or dark outside. It was always night in the cellar. Then again, during the day, you could always run out into the garden, out into the light. At night, on the other hand, it was dark *everywhere*, even outside, and ghosts lurked in every corner. Ghosts that no grown-up could see. Ghosts that were just waiting to sink their claws into the neck of an eleven-year-old boy.

Still, he just couldn't help but stare, entranced, down into the far end of the cellar where the light faded away.

The door!

It was open!

There was a gaping black opening between the dark green wall and the door. And behind it was the lab, dark like Darth Vader's Death Star.

His heart beat in his throat. Gabriel wiped his clammy, trembling hands on his pyjamas – his favourite pyjamas with Luke Skywalker on the front.

The long, dark crack of the door drew him in as if by magic. He slowly placed his bare foot on the first step. The wood of the cellar stairs felt rough and creaked as if it were trying to give him away. But he knew that they wouldn't hear him. Not as long as they were fighting behind the closed kitchen door. It was a bad one. Worse than normal. And it frightened him. Good that David wasn't there, he thought. Good that he'd taken him out of harm's way. His little brother would've cried.

Then again, it would've been nice not to be alone right now in this cellar with the ghosts. Gabriel swallowed. The opening stared back at him like the gates of hell.

Go look! That's what Luke would do.

Dad would be furious if he could see him now. The lab was Dad's secret and it was secured like a fortress with a metal door and a shiny black peephole. No one else had ever seen the lab. Not even Mum.

Gabriel's feet touched the bare concrete floor of the cellar and he shuddered. First the warm wooden steps and now the cold stone.

Now or never!

Suddenly, a rumbling came through the cellar ceiling. Gabriel flinched. The noise came from the kitchen above him. It sounded like the table had been scraped across the tiles. For a moment, he considered whether he should go upstairs. Mum was up there all alone with *him* and Gabriel knew how angry he could get.

His eyes darted back to the door, glimmering in the dark. Such an opportunity might never come again.

He had stood there once before, about two years ago. That time, Dad had forgotten to lock the upper cellar door. Gabriel was nine. He had stood in the hall for a while and peered down.

In the end, curiosity triumphed. That time, he had also crept down into the cellar, entirely afraid of the ghosts, but still in complete darkness because he didn't dare turn on the light.

The peephole had glowed red like the eye of a monster.

In a mad rush, he had fled back up the stairs, back to David in their room, and crawled into his bed.

Now he was eleven. Now he stood there downstairs again and the monster eye wasn't glowing. Still, the peephole stared at him, cold and black like a dead eye. The only things reflecting in it were the dim light on the cellar stairs and him. The closer he got, the larger his face grew.

And why did it smell so disgusting?

He groped out in front of him with his bare feet and stepped in something wet and mushy. *Puke. It was puke!* That's why it smelled so disgusting. But why was there puke *here* in the first place?

He choked down his disgust and rubbed his foot clean on a dry area of the concrete floor. Some was still stuck between his toes. He would've liked a towel or a wet cloth right about now, but the lab was more important. He reached out his hand, placed it on the knob, pulled the heavy metal door open a bit more, and pressed on into the darkness. An unnatural silence enveloped him.

A deathly silence.

A sharp chemical smell crept into his nose like at the film lab where his father had once taken him after one of his days of shooting.

His heart was pounding. Much too fast, much too loud. He wished he were somewhere else, maybe with David, under the covers.

Luke Skywalker would never hide under the covers.

The trembling fingers on his left hand searched for the light switch, always expecting to find something else entirely. What if the ghosts were here? If they grabbed his arm? If he accidently reached into one's mouth and it snapped its teeth shut?

There! Cool plastic.

He flipped the switch. Three red lights lit up and bathed the room in front of him in a strange red glow. Red, like in the belly of a monster.

A chill ran up his spine all the way to the roots of his hair. He stopped at the threshold to the lab; somehow, there was a sort of invisible border that he didn't want to cross. He squinted and tried to make out the details.

The lab was larger than he had thought, a narrow space about three metres wide and seven metres deep. A heavy black curtain hung directly beside him. Someone had hastily pushed it aside.

Clothes lines were strung under the concrete ceiling with photos hanging from them. Some had been torn down and lay on the floor.

On the left stood a photo enlarger. On the right, a shelf spanned the entire wall, crammed with pieces of equipment. Gabriel's eyes widened. He recognised most of them immediately: Arri, Beaulieu, Leicina, with other, smaller cameras in between. The trade magazines that were piled up in Dad's study on the first floor were full of them. Whenever one of those magazines wound up in the bin, Gabriel fished it out, stuck it under his pillow, and read it under the covers by torchlight until his eyelids were too heavy to keep open.

Beside the cameras lay a dozen lenses, some as long as gun barrels; next to them, small cameras, cases to absorb camera operating sounds, 8- and 16-mm film cartridges, a stack of three VCRs with four monitors, and finally, two brand-new camcorders. Dad always scoffed at the things. In one of the magazines, he had read that you could film for almost two hours with the new video technology without having to change the cassette – absolutely unbelievable! On top of that, the plastic bombers didn't rattle like film cameras, but ran silently.

Gabriel's shining eyes wandered over the treasures. He wished he could show all of this to David. He immediately felt guilty. After all, this was dangerous, so it was best that he didn't get David involved. Besides, his brother had already fallen asleep. He was right to have locked the door to their room.

Suddenly, there was a loud crash. He spun around. There was no one there. No parents, no ghost. His parents were probably still quarrelling up in the kitchen.

He looked back into the lab at all of the treasures. *Come closer*, they seemed to whisper. But he was still standing on the threshold next to the curtain. Fear rose in him. He could still turn back. He had now seen the lab; he didn't have to go all the way in.

Eleven! You're eleven! Come on, don't be a chicken!

How old was Luke?

Gabriel reluctantly took two steps into the room.

What were those photos? He bent down, picked one up from the floor, and stared at the faded grainy image. A sudden feeling of disgust and a strange excitement spread through his stomach. He looked up at the photos on the clothes line. The photo directly above him attracted his eyes like a magnet. His face was hot and red, like everything else around him. He also felt a bit sick. It looked so real, so . . . or were they actors? It looked like in the movie! The columns, the walls, like in the Middle Ages, and the black clothes . . .

He tore himself away and his eyes jumped over the jumbled storage and the shelf, and finally rested on the modern VCRs with their glittering little JVC logos. The lowest one was switched on. Numbers and characters were illuminated in its shining display. Like in *Star Wars* in the cockpit of a spaceship, he thought.

As if of its own accord, Gabriel's index finger approached the buttons and pushed one. A loud click inside the device made him jump. Twice, three times, then the hum of a motor. *A cassette!* There was a cassette in the VCR! His cheeks burned. He feverishly pushed another button. The JVC responded with a rattle. Interference lines flashed across the monitor beside the VCRs. The image wobbled for a moment, and then it was there. Diffuse with flickering colour, unreal, like a window to another world.

Gabriel had been leaning forward without knowing it – and now he jerked back. His mouth went totally dry. It was the same image as in the photo! The same place, the same columns, the same people, only now they were moving. He wanted to look away, but it was impossible. He sucked the stifling air in through his gaping mouth, and then held his breath without realising it.

The images pummelled him like the popping of flashbulbs; he couldn't help but watch, mesmerised.

The cut through the black fabric of the dress.

The pale triangle on the still paler skin.

The long, tangled blond hair.

The chaos.

And then another cut – a sharp, angry motion that spread into Gabriel's guts. He suddenly felt sick and everything was spinning. The television stared at him viciously. Trembling, he found the button and switched it off.

The image collapsed with a dull thud, as if there were a black hole inside the monitor, just like in outer space. The noise was awful, but reassuring at the same time. He stared at the dark screen and the reflection of his own bright red face. A ghost stared back, eyes wide with fear.

Don't think about it! Just don't think about it . . . He stared at the photos, at the whole mess, anything but the monitor.

What you can't see isn't there!

But it was there. Somewhere in the monitor, deep inside the black hole. The VCR made a soft grinding noise. He wanted to squeeze his eyes shut and wake up somewhere else. Anywhere. Anywhere but here. He was still crouched in front of his ghostly reflection in the monitors.

Suddenly, Gabriel was overcome by the desperate desire to see something pleasant, or even just something different. As if it had a will of its own, his finger drifted towards the other monitors.

Thud. Thud. The two upper monitors flashed on. Two washed-out images crystallised, casting their steel-blue glimmer into the red light of the lab. One image showed the hall and the open cellar door; the stairs were swallowed up by darkness. The second image showed the kitchen. The kitchen – and his parents. His father's voice rasped from the speaker.

Gabriel's eyes widened.

No! Please, no!

His father shoved the kitchen table. The table legs scraped loudly across the floor. The noise carried through the ceiling, and Gabriel winced. His father threw open a drawer, reached inside and his hand re-emerged.

Gabriel stared at the monitor in horror. Blinking, he wished he were blind. Blind and deaf.

But he wasn't.

His eyes flooded with tears. The chemical smell of the lab combined with the vomit outside the door made him gag. He wished someone would come and hug him and talk it all away.

But no one would come. He was alone.

The realisation hit him with a crushing blow. *Someone had to do something.* And now *he* was the only one who could do anything.

What would Luke do?

Quietly, he crept up the cellar stairs, his bare feet no longer able to feel the cold floor. The red room behind him glowed like hell.

If only he had a lightsabre! And then, very suddenly, he thought of something much, much better than a sabre.

Chapter 1

29 Years Later
Berlin – 1 September, 11.04 p.m.

The photo hovers like a threat in the windowless cellar. Outside, the rain is raging. The old roof of the mansion groans beneath the mass of water, and there is a dim red light rotating above the front door on the half-timbered facade, lighting up the house at brief intervals.

The torch beam darts about the dark cellar hall, revealing the slashed black fabric of a sparkling dress, which dangles from a hanger. The photo pinned onto the dress looks like a piece of wallpaper from a distance; a pale, rough scrap that has absorbed the ink from the printer, leaving the colours dull, fading away.

The dress and the photo are still swaying back and forth, as if only just hung up, and the swinging makes them seem like a decorative mobile; moving but lifeless.

The photo shows a young, very thin, heartbreakingly beautiful woman. She is slender, almost boyish, her breasts are small and flat, her face frozen, expressionless.

Her very long and very blond hair is like a crumpled yellow sheet beneath her head. She is wearing the dress to which this photo is now pinned. It seems tailor-made for her; it resembles her: flowing, extravagant, useless and costly. And the front is slashed open all the way down, as if it had an open zipper.

Beneath the dress, her skin is also slashed open – with one sharp incision starting between her legs, over her pubis and up to her chest. The abdominal wall is agape, the fleshy red of the innards veiled in merciful darkness. The black dress engulfs the body like death itself. A perfect symbol, just like the place where the dress is now hanging, waiting for him to find it: Kadettenweg 107.

The torchlight is again pointed at the bulky grey box on the wall and the tarnished lock. The key fit, but was difficult to turn, as if it couldn't remember what it was supposed to do at first. Inside, there is a row of little red light bulbs. Three are broken, and they glow at irregular intervals. The tungsten filaments have corroded over the years. But that doesn't matter. The necessary bulb is glowing.

The torchlight hastily gropes its way back to the cellar stairs and up the steps. There are footprints in the beam of light, and that's a good thing. When he returns, they will guide him down the cellar stairs to the black dress. And to the photo.

All at once, he will remember. The hairs on the back of his neck will rise, and he will say to himself: this is impossible.

And yet: it is true. He will know it. Because of the cellar alone – even if it wasn't *this* cellar or *this* woman. And of course, it will be a different woman. *His* woman.

And on her birthday, too. A lovely detail!

But the best part is the way it all comes full circle. Everything started in a cellar, and it would end in a cellar.

Cellars are the vestibules of hell. And who should know that better than someone who has been burning in hell for an eternity.

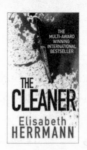

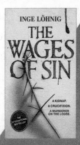